'This book is so clean and dirty . . . It is charged white space: These pages happen to you and now you're awakening, groping groggily to reconstruct. Get mixed up by it. Enter the single-wide and find some ecstasy with Faw' Richard Hell, writer and punk rock legend

'Sweet Jesus is *Young God* terrifying and great. Katherine Faw Morris's style is singular and ferocious and Nikki is one of the toughest, most electrifying, most unforgettable heroines I have ever encountered on the page. This is a furious blaze of a book that will rough you up and reorder your sense of the world and what's possible in it. It's a debut for the ages. Read it' Laura van den Berg, author of *The Isle of Youth*

'Spare [and] piquant . . . [with a] taut, concise plot' *The Millions*

'A bleak and extraordinarily assured debut' *Boston Globe*

'A short, sharp, brutal kick to the guts in fictional form – a stripped-back cliff jump of a story, brutally poetic in its minimalist vision of violence and destruction . . . a young writer to watch' *Big Issue*

'This is maybe the best first novel I've read since *Fight Club*. It comes on like a few too many pulls of Wilkes County moonshine chased with some kind of punk rock Lucinda Williams and finished with a hit of Dorothy Allison's *Bastard Out of Carolina*. Raw, spare and goddamned _____ __
you' Frank Bill, author of *Cr*___

'Like a bullet, like a bolt of ___ _____ ____
debut novel goes faster and h___ ____ _____
read this year' Stacey D'Erasr_ ____ ____ _____ _____
Wonderland

'Morris's punchy and unwavering style is absolutely of a piece with her ___ _____ _____ ___ ___ ____ Palahniuk white-trash girl-pow___

YOUNG GOD

Katherine Faw Morris

GRANTA

Granta Publications, 12 Addison Avenue, London W11 4QR

Published in Great Britain by Granta Books, 2014
This paperback published by Granta Books, 2015
First published in the US by Farrar, Straus and Giroux 2014

A CIP catalogue record for this book is available from the British
Library.

1 3 5 7 9 10 8 6 4 2

ISBN 978 1 84708 889 5
eISBN 978 1 84708 888 8

For Don

ONE

NIKKI IS ALL TO HELL. A boy jumps off the cliff in front of her. She peers over the edge, watching him go.

"Nikki."

She clenches her toes. The river is druggy and yellow and slugs next to the bottom road for miles before suddenly whipping itself into rapids and dumping, white and frothy, over the edge of this cliff.

"Nikki."

Sixty or seventy or eighty feet below is the swimming hole.

"Nikki."

"How far down is it?"

"Like a hundred feet," Wesley says.

Wesley squats near her feet. He wants to stick his dick in her. Nikki yanks tight all the bows of her bikini, hot pink. It used to be Mama's. Now Mama's too old to wear it. Nikki has been thirteen forever.

"You gonna jump?" Wesley says.

"Nikki," Mama says.

Nikki puts her hands on her hips, which are sharp like weapons.

"What?"

"You," Mama says.

Mama points at Nikki.

"Come down here."

Mama points at the book bag.

"So that me and him."

Mama flips a finger between herself and Wesley.

"Can jump."

She lets her finger drop off the cliff.

"Now."

Mama is down on the bank of the swimming hole. Nikki is dizzy as she looks back at Wesley. To her left the mountains crawl like a slow blue animal. These are just their foothills. They're lumpy and green.

A little girl died here last summer. She went off the wrong side. When they dragged the river they found her caught in a cave. Mama told this to Nikki on the way over. She was turned and watching Nikki in the backseat like she's some odd creature. Like Mama always does when she sees her. Mama's voice was rattled by the car engine. The little girl's head was smashed in, Mama said, like a basketball bitten by a dog.

"You gotta go off over there," Wesley says.

"I know," Nikki says.

"Do it then."

Wesley jabs his beer at a shrub growing out of a crack in the riverbank. This is the jumping-off place. Everywhere else is the wrong side. Nikki bends at the knees and moves her feet one by one. With a lunge she grabs the head of the shrub. Now the river flings its white froth at her. The falls roar in her ears.

"I'll go first."

"No," Nikki says.

"Just walk down on the path," Wesley says.

"No."

"Nikki," Mama says.

"God," Nikki says.

Since she is going to die she would like to be remembered, spoken of in the backs of cars in words that shudder. Nikki pictures this. She turns the shrub loose and stands up.

"Nikki."

She slips a step and then jumps.

"SHIT, SHIT, SHIT," she says.

SHE SMACKS INTO THE SWIMMING HOLE. Sinking like weights are on her feet until she remembers she can kick. She comes up gasping and touching all around her head. The river is witch-tit freezing. Shivering up at the falls she laughs to herself. It's at least two hundred feet down, she thinks.

Wesley's a stick figure flailing the long roaring drop. His shorts puff out. His yelling goes loud. His splash dumps a cold sheet of water over Nikki's head. She screams.

She swims from him. With one hand Wesley clamps her head and pushes it under and holds it there. His stomach is the hairy yellow of every other shape she can hardly see. She kicks him. She tries to pull his shorts down around his hairy yellow knees.

He slaps water in her face after he lets her up. He floats away on his back, grinning. She swims at him. She jumps up and grabs him by the skull. He squeezes her around the waist and she squeals.

"Quit it," Nikki says.

"Nikki," Mama says.

Nikki wraps her legs around Wesley. Then she squirms away from him. As soon as he's free he slips underneath. He swims for the bank. A jumper's spray lashes Nikki's back.

"Watch out," she snaps.

She swims slowly after Wesley.

"What the hell was that?"

"What?" Nikki says.

Nikki pulls herself up on the bank. It's a bunch of boulders.

"You heard me calling you," Mama says.

Nikki twists river out of her hair and doesn't look at them. Wesley's been up on the bank the whole time it took Nikki to swim here, sometimes on her back and sometimes underwater. He lounges next to Mama.

"Sit with this bag," Mama says.

Nikki sits where she's standing. Her butt bangs rock.

"You're lucky I ain't called DSS on you yet," Mama says.

"Whatever," Nikki says.

But Mama's already walking away. Nikki watches Mama walk toward the trees that hide the path. Earlier Mama made the sourest face, when Nikki came out of the bathroom wearing the pink bikini.

"What's wrong with her?" Nikki says.

Nikki leans back on her hands. Wesley flicks his cigarette over the backside of the bank where the river sneaks out.

"Watch that bag," Wesley says.

He takes his time wandering after Mama. He reaches up and folds his arms on top of his head. He could do better, Nikki thinks. He's too young, for one thing. She scoots over to the book bag. She thinks of throwing it in the water and how they would both freak out.

She feels a man staring at her. Her pulse picks up. But when she looks it's just a little boy.

"What?" she says.

Up on the cliff Mama and Wesley come out of the trees.

"Move," Nikki says.

She waves. Mama is not nearly close enough to the shrub though she is at the very edge, peering over, scratching up and down her leg.

"Mama," Nikki says.

Mama turns her back to talk to Wesley like she can't hear. Nikki rolls her eyes.

From down here the waterfall doesn't look so tall. Not more than sixty feet, Nikki thinks. Somebody jumps off with his arms swinging circles and she just shrugs. Mama is laughing at something Wesley said. Her heel slides off first.

Mama tries to catch herself but on the wrong side there is no shrub to grab. She falls down the rock wall, not the falls. Her head slams two big jags before she drops into the swimming hole with a huge splash.

All around Nikki is a sharp suck.

MEN WADE into the swimming hole. Nikki watches them. She watches the water fall behind them.

Wesley snatches the book bag and rips her up by the armpit. He's saying something.

"Let's go, let's go, let's go."

He pulls her up the path.

Nikki does not get to see Mama, if her head looks like a dog-bitten basketball or not.

SHE STARES AT HERSELF in the mirror of the medicine cabinet. She wears a bandanna tied around her mouth and nose so only her eyes show.

"OH. MY. GOD."

From the TV two girls moan. Wesley watches girl-girl porn only. He looks like he's asleep but when she puts her hand on his knee his eyes open. They're on the couch side by side.

Nikki climbs on his lap. Wesley stares at her. Because his pupils are the tiny heads of pins his eyes are the greenest green. He touches her hair.

"I like the pink."

It's Kool-Aid. Nikki kisses him. She sticks out her tongue. It's bad, the girls at the group home say, to kiss with no tongue. He moves her back and forth by the hips. After a while he unzips her shorts and has her stand up and wiggle them down.

Her panties are really the pink bottoms of the bikini but he doesn't seem to notice. She shoves them to her feet. She kicks them under the table with the bag of Mama's clothes. It's a built-in table. This is a camper.

He holds his dick in one hand. It's tall and pink.

"Oh," Nikki says.

"Come here," Wesley says.

His voice is raspy. It's dried to a husk. She straddles his lap again. She puts her hands flat on the wall behind them. She pushes with her whole weight. She bears down on him.

"Goddamn, I can feel you shaking," Wesley says.

His dick only jabs her. She wonders what's wrong with her.

"I'm harder than a fucking brick."

Nikki grits her teeth.

When she finally feels him slide inside it is not at all like she thought and much more like a jackhammer. She watches the wall behind them jerk up and down.

"Huh," Wesley says.

"Oh. My. God," the TV says.

He lets go suddenly. He pulls his dick out and flops it on her stomach where it convulses and spews warm white goo from its head.

"Ha," Wesley says.

Come, Nikki thinks. Also it's bad not to swallow come. Nikki wipes her hand up her stomach and then licks it. It tastes a little salty and mostly like nothing.

"You can stay here if you want," Wesley says.

OUT OF THE CORNER OF HER EYE she scowls at the redneck girl. The redneck girl has crunchy curls. She has big square tips. She taps them on everything. She giggles like a turkey. She's old like Mama, twenty-nine or thirty. She's been here three days. She's been the one sleeping in the bed with him.

On the couch Wesley sits between them. This girl taps her nails. She taps them on her beer can. Nikki stands up. She puts her hands on her hips. She does not have to put up with this.

"Where are you going?" Wesley says.

"I got a daddy," Nikki says.

TWO

IN HER MOUTH his name is shiny and bitter like a licked coin.

"Coy Hawkins."

It rings out.

"YOU FUCKING CUNT," Wesley yells.

He trips in the yard. The redneck girl gapes from the camper's top step. Nikki watches them in the rearview. Until they disappear around a hook in the hill.

Wesley lives near the top of his hill but not the very top. His road's dirt. It whiplashes. Dogs lunge from most places but always catch on their chains. Their different howling follows her down. One old man stares from his chair. Gas on the right, brake on the left. It's not so hard.

At the foot of Wesley's hill Nikki crosses the yellow river. It creeps by like it always will. She turns onto the bottom road, away from the falls.

The bottom road goes from dirt to gravel to tar. From falls to highway, but she's not going that far. As soon as the dirt bumps to gravel she lets off the gas. She inches along.

A car bunches behind her and honks and finally passes. She's looking for this chicken house with its windows shattered. When she sees it she almost turns around. Just past it she cuts a steep left onto a road that's not marked.

There are no barking dogs because nobody lives on this hill until you get to him. And Crystal and them. On the way up there are zero houses. There are PRIVATE PROPERTY—NO TRESPASSING signs on every tenth trunk. It's twisty and sheer. It's rutty as if driving up ribs. A chill runs through Nikki's teeth.

She hasn't been up here in years. When she's run away it's been to Mama. But at the very top of this hill, above the big house, that's where her money is buried.

In the middle of the road, like a deer, is a little boy on a bicycle.

NIKKI SLAMS THE BRAKES. The little boy grabs the side mirror with both hands.

"I almost killed you," she says.

"Who you?" he says.

He leans on the mirror to look inside. He is nine or ten. Nikki stares at him, at his crooked ears.

"I ain't never seen you before," he says.

"Levi?" she says.

He leans back to squint at her.

"It's Nikki," she says.

"Who?"

She doesn't have time for this. She smashes the gas and his hand snaps from the mirror.

In the rearview she watches him coming up behind. He has to stand on his pedals to climb. The last time she saw him he could barely walk. She glares at him. He must have been here all these years.

She turns the last bend. The road levels off, the trees part. She nearly screeches the brakes again.

On the top of the hill there is one yard and two houses. Crystal's house is boarded up because Crystal's in prison. But the big house is boarded up, too. Its doors and windows are nailed shut with plywood. In the wild yard are two trailers now. Two single-wides.

She rolls to a stop next to a plain black pickup. She sits and stares at it.

She should leave. This is the first place DSS will check. A door squeals. Coy Hawkins comes out of the trailer parked in front of the big house. He stands on the top step. Nikki gets out of the car.

He looks like he's supposed to. He looks skinny and slick-headed. She waits for him to grin but he just crosses his arms over his chest. She remembers her pink hair.

"It's me," she says.

"What are you doing up here?" Coy Hawkins says.

Her face twists.

"Mama died."

Coy Hawkins scratches his jaw.

"At the falls," Nikki says.

"That was your mama?" Levi says.

He circles her on his bike.

"I heard they pulled a body out," Coy Hawkins says.

She tries to think of what else to say. A girl comes out of the trailer. A girl who looks like a mouse. But with her hair bleached blond and piled on top of her head. She stands next to him on the top step and Coy Hawkins lifts his arm and drapes it around her neck.

"Angel?" Nikki says.

"What's she doing up here?" Angel says.

AT THE GROUP HOME Angel never said anything. She was so quiet she barely existed. She lights an extra-skinny cigarette. Nikki can't stop staring. She looks so different.

"What happened to your glasses?"

"I don't wear them no more," Angel says.

"You drove that car up here?" Coy Hawkins says.

The three of them are sitting in the trailer's kitchen. They're sitting in folding chairs around a card table. It's dim and dusty. There's a skillet, a coffeepot, and three ashtrays. Coy Hawkins smokes regular-sized cigarettes. He smokes Kool Kings in a hard box.

"Yeah," Nikki says.

"DSS was up here the other day."

Nikki looks at him.

"What did you tell them?"

"I told them I ain't seen you because I ain't," Coy Hawkins says.

He taps his lighter on the table.

"Then."

Nikki looks at Angel.

"What did you tell them about her?"

The only thing Angel is wearing is one of Coy Hawkins's shirts. The buttons are skewed, a few of them. Coy Hawkins smirks.

Angel scrunches her nose.

"Is she staying here?" Angel says.

The last time Nikki saw Coy Hawkins his eyes were big black beads. He was smoking crack then. Today they're just blue. Nikki shrugs. She guesses she is staying.

She grabbed the book bag before she left.

"I got like five hundred Roxies if y'all want some," she says.

"Do what?" Angel says.

"In the car," Nikki says.

"Where the hell you get them?" Angel says.

"Wesley Harrell."

Coy Hawkins leans back until his chair hits the wall.

"Well, let's see them," he says.

SHE EXPECTED HIM to sell them first. Call somebody. However that works. Nikki didn't snort any. Angel's nodding on the couch. Coy Hawkins is slumped in a reclining chair. Nikki stands at its foot, completely alert.

THIS TRAILER is the tube kind. It goes kitchen, living room, hallway, bathroom, bedroom. Nikki starts there.

The carpet's green. The headboard of the bed is cut into cubbyholes and stuffed with anything: beer cans, clothes, ashtrays, hair spray, tissues. The closet is mirrored. Nikki looks at herself in it. She makes a face. She twirls her pink hair on top of her head. Then she rolls her eyes.

The closet slides open. On its floor is a pile of boots. Some trash bags. She dumps one out and dresses slink to her feet. They are bright and shiny. They have see-through parts or leopard spots or laces up and down the sides. Nikki pictures Angel trying them on and Coy Hawkins buying them. Nikki steps back to see what she's wearing. She snaps fray off her shorts and makes a face again.

Also there are some shoe boxes but the only thing in them are poisonous packets.

The bathroom is off the hall. It's small and linoleum. The mirror doesn't open. Plugged into the wall is an electric shaver. Nikki finds Angel's stuff under the sink in another trash bag. She has a hair dryer and a flatiron. She has a whole pouch of makeup. Nikki opens a thing of glitter. She rips back the shower curtain. If she squints she sees bleached blond hairs plastered to the stall. They're in the sink, too, and on the walls.

Nikki lifts the lid off the toilet tank and peers in.

In the living room there's the couch and the reclining chair, a coffee table and a boxy TV with rabbit ears that says NO SIG-NAL on the screen. The couch is plaid. Nikki flips up the skirt and pulls out mail and coffee cups. She checks the pockets of Coy Hawkins's chair.

When she sits back on her heels Angel's looking at her.

"Hey," Nikki says.

Angel's eyes close.

Nikki opens all the kitchen cabinets. She cracks the stove and microwave. She stares into the refrigerator. There's a bag of potato chips in the vegetable crisper. The freezer has pounds of ground beef and a jar of liquor with a peach in the bottom. Nikki sips some. The moonshine burns a path down her throat to her heart. She bares her teeth.

"Uh," she says.

She sits at the card table to think. Coy Hawkins used to be the biggest coke dealer in the county. But if there are kilos in here she can't find them.

NIKKI BRINGS THE LIQUOR into the living room. She flops the rabbit ears until a channel comes in. She nudges Angel with her knee. Angel cuts her teeth and bats at Nikki limply. She curls to the other side of the couch. Nikki sits down.

A phone is on the coffee table. There's no service up here. Nikki goes to photos. The first photo is of Angel against one of the fake wood walls of the trailer, naked, with her fingers between her legs. She is shaved like a porn star. The phone clatters when Nikki drops it but they are not disturbed.

She watches TV sitting up. She watches TV lying down. She dips her finger in liquor and sets it on fire.

Coy Hawkins opens his eyes.

"Is that my brandy?" he says.

His voice is raspy, dried to a husk.

"Yeah," Nikki says.

Angel's cigarette ash drips in her lap. Nikki eats the peach off a fork, watching it.

Nikki smokes a cigarette in front of the mirrored closet. A Kool King. The third one in a row makes her run to the bathroom and puke in the toilet.

The hall ripples. She takes a wrong step and runs into the wall. She wonders if this is shitfaced or just drunk.

She stares at him. Coy Hawkins's shirt is unbuttoned and he has no new tattoos and that means nobody tried to fuck with him in prison. He still has Mama's name on his chest. It's over his left nipple. He did it himself with a needle and ink and it's thin and green. She rests the jar on the arm of his chair.

She pulls the blue pills out of the book bag. They're in a Ziploc stuffed in a sock wrapped in a towel so they don't rattle. Nikki thinks about hiding them in the freezer, behind the meat.

She sits on the couch beside Angel again.

"I'm sorry about your mama," Angel says.

Nikki looks at her. Angel is scratching up and down her arms.

"It's fine," Nikki says.

Angel shrugs.

Gunshots. Hunters, Nikki tells herself.

When she closes her eyes the whole world spins.

SHE DREAMS OF NOTHING, which is her favorite dream, and inside of her is a low buzz.

WHEN SHE FINDS THAT DOG that shit in her mouth last night she's going to kill it. Before she didn't really know what that meant. She rolls her forehead in her hand. She gets up from the couch and the jar slams her toes.

"Fuck," Nikki says.

OUTSIDE A CAR RUMBLES. Nikki sits up. She touches a crust on her cheek. Coy Hawkins walks through the living room with a gun.

Angel's foot is on Nikki's knee. Nikki throws it off. She bangs out the front door after him.

Wesley's in the yard, in front of an idling car. He's with some man Nikki's never seen. Probably everybody calls him Bubba. He's tall and totally round. Coy Hawkins is pointing the gun at them. They have their hands up but only halfway.

"Man, I heard you were out again," Wesley says.

"What I tell you?" Bubba says.

"What do you want?" Coy Hawkins says.

Wesley leans to the side.

"Nikki," he says.

She's behind Coy Hawkins, on the bottom trailer step. She juts her hip. She wishes she were wearing one of Angel's dresses. Wesley leans back to Coy Hawkins.

"I been looking for your daughter. She took a stash of blues off me and my fucking car."

Coy Hawkins looks over his shoulder. Nikki bunches up her face.

"No, I didn't," she says.

Coy Hawkins sighs. He looks at Wesley again.

"Grab them pills," Coy Hawkins says.

Nikki has to think about this. She thinks she's still drunk. There is a long pause.

"Do what?"

"Did I stutter?" Coy Hawkins says.

Inside Angel's up on her knees. She's splitting the blinds with her fingers.

"What's going on?" Angel says.

Nikki pulls the book bag from under the couch.

Down the stairs the sun beats her head. It makes her feel sick. When she tries to hand the bag to Coy Hawkins he flicks the gun at Wesley instead. Briefly Nikki closes her eyes and then she opens them again.

She walks up to him. She wants to die.

"Here," she says.

Wesley doesn't even look at her. He unzips the book bag. He unwraps the towel and pulls off the sock. He looks over her head.

"It's light," Wesley says.

"Is it?" Coy Hawkins says.

Wesley sniffs. He chins at the car that's parked beside the black pickup.

"The keys in there?" Wesley says.

"Car's staying," Coy Hawkins says.

Wesley stares at Coy Hawkins. Then he nods. He nods for a while. He looks at Bubba.

"All right," he says.

Bubba nods, too.

"Fucking Coy Hawkins," he says.

Squealing off they kick up grass. Around the bend trees swallow them. Nikki turns to him. He drops the gun to his side.

"You can always use another vehicle," Coy Hawkins says.

He goes up the steps.

In a daze Nikki looks at the yard. She looks at Levi on his bike, and beyond that to the trailer in front of Crystal's house, where in the living room window two blinds are slit.

ANGEL'S FACE is like somebody switched on the light. She has cat's eyes and red lips. She is wearing one of those dresses that laces up the sides. It sucks to her. It makes her nipples pop out like two buttons.

Her hair is huge. She walks from the hall in a pair of rickety high heels. She leans over to grab her stupid cigarettes and a sugary cloud of perfume blows at Nikki on the couch.

"What?" Angel says.

"I can see your titties," Nikki says.

Coy Hawkins comes out of the hall, too. He snaps at Angel.

"Get in the truck," he says.

"She ain't coming?" Angel says.

Coy Hawkins says nothing. Angel crosses her arms over her chest. She has to bend her knees to walk. She glares at Nikki until the door slams behind her.

"Where are y'all going?" Nikki says.

"Out," Coy Hawkins says.

"When are y'all coming back?"

"Later."

"What if they come back for the car?" Nikki says.

"They probably won't."

Coy Hawkins is standing in front of the coffee table. He's buttoning his shirt.

"You ain't like you used to be."

He stops for a second. He looks at her.

"Neither are you," he says.

After he's gone she stares at the blank TV. She listens to the engine struggle to rev on the truck and finally catch.

LEVI SKIDS in front of her. He yanks his handlebars to pop a wheelie and smashes on his side. His bike clanks on top of him.

"Ow," he says.

Nikki steps around him. The big house is gray though it should be white. It looks skinny. It looks like a place the fire department would burn down for practice. She climbs onto the front porch and her foot falls through dry rot.

"Fuck," she says.

"You're Nikki," Levi says.

Nikki says nothing.

"My mama's your daddy's sister."

Over her shoulder Levi is rubbing his elbow. She pulls her foot from the porch.

"Half sister," Nikki says.

"We're cousins," Levi says.

"Half cousins."

Behind the big house is random trash like toilets and mattresses. Nikki weaves through it. As she walks the grass grows. White moths fly at her face and she slaps them away. When she gets to the far edge of the yard it's up to her waist. Woods hide the very top of the hill. The only way up is the deer cut.

Nikki wheels around.

"Quit following me," she says.

"I ain't," Levi says.

Its mouth is overgrown. It's a mess of brush and giant weeds, like all the deer left when Nikki did. Up the deer cut is where her money's buried.

She wanders back toward the big house. The plywood is loose on one of the back windows. A single board hangs from a nail. She swings it with her finger. She wonders what's still in there. She looks at Levi. He is right behind her.

"See?" she says.

"What?" he says.

He squints the other way. Nikki puts her hands on her hips.

"You stay with your grandmama?" Nikki says.

"Yeah," Levi says.

Levi's grandmama is not Nikki's grandmama. She is only Crystal's mama, not Coy Hawkins's. Nikki looks at the other trailer, the one in front of Crystal's house, which is smaller than the big house, with no upstairs. In the living room window the blinds are flat. Nikki purses her lips.

"My mama's in prison," Levi says.

"I know," Nikki says.

He is irritating her.

"Why you think my mama's still in prison and your daddy ain't?"

"I don't care."

Every time she comes outside he's going to be lurking, she thinks. He's digging a hole with his heel.

"Because your daddy's a rat," Levi says.

There are old bricks by her feet, what used to be the chimney. She picks one up and throws it at him and it thuds. Levi sits down. His chest pumps up and down with his breathing.

NIKKI TAKES A LONG PINK SHOWER. Kool-Aid runs the crooks of her arms and the insides of her thighs. She bends bowlegged in the stall. She shaves off her pubic hair and it kinks to the drain. She goes into the bedroom. She stands bare in front of the mirrored closet and scrutinizes herself. She is so much prettier than Angel.

SHE HEARS SOMETHING. A rumble. She runs to the kitchen and grabs a knife but it turns out to be nothing.

"SHE'S WEARING MY DRESS," Angel says.

Nikki pulls up the elastic top of one of them with leopard spots. Angel looks outraged. Coy Hawkins hardly looks at all. They just walked in. It's morning.

"Will you tell her she can't wear my clothes?" Angel says.

Coy Hawkins sits in his chair. He fiddles with the crank until the footrest shoots up.

"Jesus Christ," Angel says.

She sits next to Nikki. She flicks the bikini bow at Nikki's neck.

"You ain't even supposed to wear a bra with it."

"Don't touch me," Nikki says.

"Get up," Coy Hawkins says.

They both look at him. He looks drunk.

"Angel, get up," Coy Hawkins says.

"Why?" Angel says.

He snaps like ten times.

When Angel stands up Nikki smells something foul. Nikki looks at her. She is holding her high heels by the hooks of her fingers and they seriously reek.

Angel kicks Nikki climbing over her. She sits on the arm of Coy Hawkins's chair.

"No," Coy Hawkins says.

"What, I'm supposed to sit on the floor?"

Coy Hawkins tries to light the filter end of a cigarette.

"Hello?" Angel says.

"You hear something?"

Coy Hawkins says this only to Nikki. Nikki stares at them. Angel's hair is back on top of her head. The tails of her cat's eyes are sweated off and her lips are no longer red. They look puffy.

Angel bumps by Nikki's knees. She sits down on the couch again.

"Get up," Coy Hawkins says.

"No," Angel says.

Nikki wonders if he took her to the steakhouse where you get to throw your peanut shells on the floor.

"Get up," Coy Hawkins says.

Also he probably bought her breakfast. Nikki had potato chips.

"I stutter?" Coy Hawkins says.

"Yes."

"Get up," Nikki says.

"Do what?" Angel says.

Angel looks at her.

"Your feet stink," Nikki says.

"What?"

"They're rank."

Angel stares at Nikki. Her face is red. Her mouth is open. Nikki waits. Angel's eyes shift. She looks at Coy Hawkins.

"This is fucking bullshit," Angel says.

She throws her high heels at the wall. She stands up and goes around to the far side of the coffee table and sits on the floor. When Nikki looks at Coy Hawkins he's laughing so hard no sound comes out.

THEY ARE PRESSED against the bathroom sink. Coy Hawkins is pulling Angel's hair and Angel's hand is down Coy Hawkins's jeans. Nikki stands there a second too long. He turns his head and sees.

WHEN NIKKI TAKES OFF THE BIKINI TOP her nipples pop like two buttons, too. She walks into the living room. She feels him watching. She fights the urge to cross her arms over her chest. After she sits down on the couch she waits awhile. Then she looks at him.

"What?" Nikki says.

Coy Hawkins shakes his head.

Nikki stares at the TV and pretends to care. Angel's asleep beside her. She's made herself into a tiny ball. She's wearing one of his shirts again.

"You were just a little girl the last time I seen you," Coy Hawkins says.

"I know," Nikki says.

"You don't remember back then. Not really."

"Yes, I do."

"You remember what your mama told you to."

She looks at him. He's drinking a cup of coffee. He takes a sip.

Later they are all in the kitchen. Nikki and Angel are sitting in folding chairs and Coy Hawkins is pacing. He's smoking a cigarette. He's holding an ashtray. He stops and looks at Nikki.

"You got any better shoes?"

Nikki looks at her flip-flops.

"No," she says.

He points his cigarette at Angel.

"Find her something," he says.

Angel has his shirt stretched over her knees. She drops her feet to the floor. She smirks at Nikki.

"Are we going somewhere?" Nikki says.

"Out," Coy Hawkins says.

"Out," Angel says.

ANGEL SITS IN THE BITCH SEAT. Around left bends they both slide across the pickup's bench and bunch against Coy Hawkins. Nikki laughs. Coy Hawkins turns up the stereo, louder, louder, louder, until both Nikki and Angel scream.

AT THE OTHER END of the bottom road is the highway. It's a long-looping highway. It's really just a road that's always tar. It leads to town. It takes forever to get there: twenty minutes. The whole time is dropping down but gradually. Nikki hardly feels it.

Along the way it's mostly churches. The old ones are brick. The ones that got pissed off and split off from them are in storefronts. The ones that got pissed off and split off from them are in abandoned gas stations.

Very close to town there's the twenty-four-hour Coffee House and the Food Lion and the big cemetery. Otherwise it's trees.

Right now it's dark. The trees fly by as inky fringe. In Nikki's mind there is a certain glittering blackness.

The town is cut by a river. Not the yellow one but what it flows into. The south side of the town is flatter. It's where Walmart is and the people who just got money live. The north side of town is steeper. It's where the people who've always had money live and also all the black people. There are Mexicans everywhere now.

On the north side of town, at the stoplight that turns for the group home, Nikki doesn't breathe. Coy Hawkins gases it as soon as it goes green. Past an empty building where a gun-and-pawn used to be he makes a left onto another highway. He heads back into the county. The county is anywhere that's not town. Nikki turns to look at them. Angel's chewing gum.

"Where are we going?" she says.

The highway spits them out to the southeast, into a different county. Nikki clutches the door handle as the pickup merges, rattling, onto an interstate. Tractor-trailers whip by. Headlights spot her eyes. It is six lanes, stick-straight. Nikki stares at everything. Sometimes she flinches. The road signs say CHARLOTTE.

"Where are we going?" she says.

Seventy miles.

Sixty miles.

Fifty miles.

Forty miles to Charlotte Coy Hawkins takes an exit. He exits onto a road that is all gas stations, drive-thrus, and motels. They march along either side, on and on. It is super bright. Coy Hawkins pulls into a motel's lot. It's a two-floor motel with a balcony. He parks around back and gets out and walks around front. Nikki squints, watching him go.

"Where are we?" Nikki says.

"Where do you think?" Angel says.

COY HAWKINS opens his fist. In his hand are chalky white pills like generic Oxy.

"What's that?"

"Rolls," Angel says.

"Oxy?" Nikki says.

"Ecstasy."

Nikki looks at her.

"What's it do?"

"It eats holes in your brain."

"No, it don't."

Angel nods at Nikki.

"Let me get one," Nikki says.

Ecstasy is a real drug like coke. Any person with a prescription can't get it. Coy Hawkins gives Angel two of them. He eats two himself. Now his palm is empty.

"No," Coy Hawkins says.

Angel laughs.

Nikki cuts her teeth. She slumps in the seat. Angel reaches over to throw her gum out the window and presses her hand against Nikki.

"Get off me," Nikki says.

When Angel lets go a pill is stuck to Nikki's thigh. Nikki drops her fingers over it. She stares at the back of the motel. Angel leans back. Nikki bends down as if to scratch her leg and swallows the roll instead.

Coy Hawkins gives Angel a key card.

"Six," he says.

"Why can't we go to the Super 8?" Angel says.

Coy Hawkins looks at his phone.

"I thought we were never coming back here," Angel says.

"Run to the store, get me a pack of cigarettes," Coy Hawkins says.

"Can I go, too?" Nikki says.

Coy Hawkins glances at her.

"Hurry up," he says.

Nikki teeters in the high heels. They're not as shiny as Angel's pair but they don't stink either. Nikki has to bend her knees and cross her arms over her chest. Angel stops at the edge of the service road.

In a minute Nikki catches up. Tractor-trailers shudder their hair.

"Run when I say to," Angel says.

Nikki looks at her.

"No," Nikki says.

"Run."

Nikki sprints behind Angel across two lanes of traffic. They pause in the middle. Then two more lanes. A few times Nikki closes her eyes. On the other side she almost pukes.

"Come on," Angel says.

They walk through parking lots, one bleeding into the next. Some of the drivers honk and Nikki looks but Angel just ignores them.

"Where did you meet him?"

"What?"

"Coy Hawkins."

Angel turns around. She walks backward into the gas station's pool of light.

"Online," Angel says.

Inside they turn the sunglasses display. Men watch them.

Nikki crosses her arms over her chest. Then she flips her hair to one side. Angel doesn't seem to care.

At the register Angel shows a strange girl's license.

"Kool Kings in a hard box," she says.

She puts a roll of bubble gum next to Coy Hawkins's cigarettes.

"You're fifty cents short," the register man says.

Angel pats her dress like it could hide anything. She cocks one hip into the counter.

"I don't got it," she says.

"You don't got fifty cents?"

Angel shrugs. The register man sighs. He has a ponytail. He chins at the door.

Nikki teeters after her. They go through parking lots chewing gum. They pull down stolen sunglasses from the tops of their heads.

"You used to be so quiet."

"What?" Angel says.

"You never talked."

"I'm like three years older than you."

"Two years," Nikki says.

At the edge of the service road Angel grabs Nikki's hand. Angel's hand is hot. Nikki is freezing.

"Run," Angel says.

Tractor-trailer horns swoop their ears. Their sunglasses are streaked by flashing brights. Nikki feels giddy. She thinks the ecstasy has started.

Back in the motel lot Coy Hawkins gives Angel the key card again. He passes it through the pickup window.

"Six," he says.

"Come on," Angel says.

"Not her," Coy Hawkins says.

"Why not?"

"Just you."

Angel drops Nikki's hand.

"You bitch," Angel says.

"What?" Nikki says.

"I should have never gave you that roll."

Coy Hawkins rips the sunglasses off Angel's face. Angel dips from his hand. She stalks off across the parking lot. Nikki just stands there.

She watches Angel use the key card to open a motel room on the bottom floor. It has pleated curtains. It has a 6 painted on the cinder block wall outside the door. Nikki puts her hand on the windowsill.

"What's she doing?"

"She's got dates," Coy Hawkins says.

"Dates?"

Nikki is startled when she looks at him. Coy Hawkins is wearing Angel's sunglasses. They're the same white plastic as hers.

"Dates?"

"Get in the truck, Nikki."

"YOU'RE A PIMP?"

Coy Hawkins says nothing.

"Why?" Nikki says.

"I got shit to buy. Why you think anybody works?"

A man gets out of a car and knocks on Angel's door. He's plain looking. The room opens a sliver and he slips inside. Coy Hawkins taps his phone on the steering wheel. Nikki was not expecting this. She doesn't know how to act.

Her knees don't feel like they belong to her. She looks at her hands resting on them. She looks at the pickup bench between them. Something warm bursts inside her brain like it's being eaten.

"Oh," Nikki says.

ROLLING. Before she didn't get what that meant.

"IS IT BECAUSE OF THE ECONOMY?"

"What?"

"That you're a pimp?"

Coy Hawkins laughs with his head thrown back.

"What?" Nikki says.

She laughs, too. Though she doesn't think it's funny.

"You used to be the biggest coke dealer in the county."

Coy Hawkins rests his elbow on the bench seat. He looks at her.

"You were," she says.

"Everybody's on pills now," Coy Hawkins says.

"So?"

"This is my new thing. This is the future."

Nikki looks out at the motel parking lot. Her teeth are grinding.

"What?" she says.

WHEN COY HAWKINS'S PHONE VIBRATES all of
Nikki's veins shake.

"YOU DON'T LOOK NOTHING LIKE HER."

"Like who?"

"Your mama," Coy Hawkins says.

"I know. I look like you."

Coy Hawkins is doing something weird with his mouth. Nikki doesn't want to talk anymore.

"You never called me, not once," she says.

"I was in prison," Coy Hawkins says.

"I was in the group home," Nikki says.

Coy Hawkins puts his hand on Nikki's alien knee, briefly.

HE SAID TO GET SOMETHING TO DRINK. She slides a six-pack onto the counter.

"ID?"

Nikki looks down at her dress that can't hide anything. She feels nothing when she bangs her hip into Plexiglas.

"I forgot it," she says.

The register man gestures over her head.

"Next."

She runs across the service road on her own. She almost gets hit. She feels so fuzzy. She climbs back into the pickup. Coy Hawkins looks at her. She's empty-handed.

"He carded me."

"For water?" Coy Hawkins says.

NIKKI IS THINKING so many things she can't remember though she just thought them.

This bubble gum is dull in her mouth. It has zero taste. She wonders how long she's been chewing it.

She thinks if either one of them moves, Coy Hawkins or her, she will panic and vomit everywhere.

A different man comes out of Angel's room.

"THE MONEY'S STILL THERE?"

She waits a long time for him to say *yeah, it is.*

When she finally looks at Coy Hawkins he's asleep. Nikki won't ever sleep again. She stares at him in disbelief.

THE SUN RISES. It rises over gas stations and drive-thrus and motels. It rises over parking lots. It rises over sparse trees and pale grass. On the horizon there are no mountains, foggy and looming, like they don't even exist. Nikki feels uneasy. This is what happens when the foothills run out. The world goes flat.

Angel gets in the pickup. Whore, Nikki thinks.

"Cash," Coy Hawkins says.

"Y'all should really take off them sunglasses," Angel says.

"WHAT'S THAT SMELL?"

It's not Angel's feet. It's a thin, yellow-green stench.

"Chicken shit," Angel says.

"What?" Nikki says.

"You ain't never been out of the county?"

So, she thinks.

"You don't smell it if you don't leave," Angel says.

"It's fertilizer," Coy Hawkins says.

He looks at her out of the corner of his eye. From the bitch seat Nikki watches the sign for the county shoot by. It looks like a car smashed into it. Her whole body relaxes.

In town it's still early. The stoplights are blinking. Coy Hawkins rolls through the group-home light and the other two and then they are back on the highway that cuts up into the north part of the county.

They start to climb. They start to wind. Nikki tilts her head back on the bench and stares at the pickup ceiling. This ecstasy will never end.

This highway goes all the way to Virginia.

The bottom road breaks from tar to gravel with a thump. The road up his hill is so steep it slams her back in her seat. When Coy Hawkins pulls into his yard Nikki looks at the trees. They make a ring around her that is deep, dark green. Above them, to her left, the mountains are huge and blue.

Coy Hawkins and Angel get out and leave her there. She smells nothing. She thinks it's going to be okay.

ANGEL OPENS HER MOUTH in an *O*. Nikki sits beside her, in front of the mirrored closet, watching her. After Angel's done she looks at Nikki. Nikki shrugs. Angel grabs Nikki's face.

The eyeliner is cold and squirmy. Nikki's scalp prickles and she wishes it would always. When Angel lets go Nikki opens her eyes. Nikki's mouth twitches up in the mirror.

"You were so fucked up last night," Angel says.

"No, I wasn't," Nikki says.

Angel curls into a ball and mimes shivering all over. She laughs. In the mirror Nikki's new cat's eyes twinkle. She feels like shit. She feels like every nutrient in her body has been leached.

"It was fun," Nikki says.

Angel turns lipstick out of a tube. It goes on bright red. Angel sticks a finger in her mouth and drags it out between her teeth. She passes the lipstick to Nikki. She reaches out and shakes Nikki's knee.

"You're so skinny," Angel says.

"So are you," Nikki says.

Nikki puts a finger in her mouth and pulls it out.

"Can you give blood?"

"Do what?"

"I can't," Angel says.

Nikki's lips are so red. She pushes them together and parts them again.

"I never gave blood," she says.

"You got to be at least a hundred and ten so you don't black out."

Nikki looks at the two of them. For one thing Angel's face is not great.

"I'm like ninety-five," Angel says.

Nikki looks at Angel's hand on her knee.

"I'm like ninety-one," Nikki says.

Angel pushes up the bottom of Nikki's dress.

"Are you wearing a bathing suit?"

"What?" Nikki says.

One of Angel's fingers is holding the elastic of the bikini bottom away from Nikki's skin. Nikki clamps her legs shut.

Angel smirks. Angel nods at the bed where Coy Hawkins is sleeping. The covers are on the floor. He's half-wrapped in the fitted sheet.

"He's just waiting to see who's gonna pay the most money for you," Angel says.

"What?" Nikki says.

"It's called the high bid. Because you're a virgin."

"I ain't a virgin."

Angel puts on Nikki's white sunglasses.

"You act like one," Angel says.

"I don't gotta work for him. He's my daddy," Nikki says.

Angel turns to look at Nikki.

"That don't matter."

NIKKI OPENS THE COOLER DOOR. A man opens the door beside her. She closes hers and leans against the glass. She puts a hand on her hip. When the man closes his door she looks at him with cat's eyes and red lips. She shakes in the gas station's air conditioning. He swings his beer at her as if he's about to say something.

"Stop staring," Nikki snaps.

She hurries down the aisle with her pulse pounding. She looks over her shoulder to make sure he's not following. She grabs a bag of chips.

"CHIP?" Coy Hawkins says.

"I ain't a virgin," Nikki says.

Coy Hawkins takes his time chewing. He licks his fingers.

"You should be."

Nikki glares at him. She doesn't know how he can eat. The thought of food is the thought of chewed cardboard in her mouth. She looks at the back of the motel.

"All you do now is sit in parking lots all night."

Coy Hawkins puts a chip in his mouth.

TWO GIRLS COME DOWN THE STAIRS from the motel's second floor. They're black girls in tight dresses. They're in tall high heels and they have to hold on to the railing. Nikki watches them. She decides they're whores, too.

They get in a mauve car. Coy Hawkins turns the key in the pickup.

"Where are we going?" Nikki says.

The pickup goes through the parking lot behind the mauve car. They both make a left. Nikki looks over her shoulder at the motel.

"What about Angel?"

"She's busy," Coy Hawkins says.

The gas station flies by. It's late and the service road is dead but Coy Hawkins rides the girls' tail.

Nikki stares at their mauve trunk for a while.

"Are we following them?"

"Yeah," Coy Hawkins says.

She looks at him.

"Why?"

"They're the gorilla pimp's girls."

"Who?" Nikki says.

"The gorilla pimp."

"What's a gorilla pimp?"

"It means he beats them."

"Them two girls?"

"Broke arms hanging out of the socket, shit like that."

Nikki stares at him.

"You ain't a gorilla pimp?" she says.

He does that weird thing with his mouth. He's rolling again. Nikki's not. This time Angel didn't share. The interstate swoops overhead.

"Do they know we're following them?" Nikki says.

"I don't think so," Coy Hawkins says.

The mauve car's brakes flash. The girls make a right and so does the pickup. The road lamps go out. It's pitch-black and they go faster through the dark. Nikki gets that wild feeling like she always used to have with him.

The mauve car pulls into a courtyard made by four buildings. They're low and brick and they dead-end the road. The pickup pulls in, too. Coy Hawkins parks next to the girls.

"Come on," he says.

Nikki is holding on to the bench seat.

"Is the gorilla pimp the high bid?"

"The what?"

Coy Hawkins turns to look at her and his eyes are the size of saucers.

"Angel said you're waiting to see who's gonna pay the most money for me because you think I'm a virgin and it don't matter that you're my daddy."

The way Coy Hawkins laughs makes her put her hands in her lap.

"And you believed her?"

"No," Nikki says.

"Come on," he says.

The girls are already out of the car. They are walking backward across the courtyard staring at Nikki and Coy Hawkins. They have the same tattoo. It cinches their necks. It says something.

"Who the fuck are you?" the skinny girl says.

"Were you fucking following us?" the other girl says.

Nikki trails behind him. She scans the apartments all around. In the middle of the courtyard there is grass and a gazebo and boys who were sitting in lawn chairs but are now standing up. She yanks down the hem of her dress. She crosses her arms over her chest.

"Your daddy in?" Coy Hawkins says.

Nikki looks at him.

"Who?" the skinny girl says.

When Nikki stops so does Coy Hawkins. He reaches back and grabs Nikki's hand. He lifts it up in his.

"I brung him this," Coy Hawkins says.

The girls cut their teeth. The boys sit down.

"He inside," the other girl says.

NIKKI SCREAMS.

COY HAWKINS gets Nikki by the hair. He scrapes her across the courtyard on her hands and knees. He drags her into an apartment. All the blood rushes out of her head.

They're in this living room. It's air-conditioned and freezing. A man saunters down a hall and she strains to see him. He's wearing sweatpants. He bends down to look at her. He tilts his head at Nikki and grins.

"You're the gorilla pimp?" Nikki says.

The girls snicker. The gorilla pimp flops over the arm of a love seat. He's smaller than one of them and prettier than both of them. His chest is narrow and hairless. He has diamond studs in his ears. His nails are shiny. She can't think.

He chins above her head.

"Cletus, how you know where I live at?" he says.

"I been sitting outside that motel your girls like for two nights," Coy Hawkins says.

"He fucking followed us," the other girl says.

"He creepy," the skinny girl says.

"That motel where you tried to steal my other girl. You remember that?" Coy Hawkins says.

The gorilla pimp smirks. The girls are standing on either side of him.

"Man, you still tight about that?"

Nikki stares at the carpet. It's beige. It waves.

"That was like last month," the gorilla pimp says.

"I ain't a virgin," Nikki says.

"Shut up," Coy Hawkins says.

The girls laugh. She's going to pass out. The gorilla pimp turns on the TV. He gestures at her with the remote.

"I'll give you ten for this one," he says.

Nikki pukes on the carpet.

"Did she just puke on my carpet?"

"Oh my God," the skinny girl says.

"She about to get it," the other girl says.

Coy Hawkins pulls Nikki to the love seat. He lets go of her hair. Her eyes dart. She tries to read the girls' necks. The gorilla pimp's not their real daddy. He's way too young, she thinks.

"I'm his daughter," Nikki shrieks.

Coy Hawkins flicks out a knife. He slashes the gorilla pimp's face, both sides.

The girls scream. They scream so loud Nikki covers her ears. The gorilla pimp puts a hand to his cheek and then he looks at it.

Coy Hawkins shoves Nikki out the door. In the courtyard the boys are gone from their chairs.

WHEN THEY TURN ONTO THE SERVICE ROAD all the lights flare back, super bright.

"It ain't just sitting in parking lots," Coy Hawkins says.

Nikki stares at him.

"WHOSE BLOOD IS THAT?"

Angel's in the bitch seat. Coy Hawkins turns out of the motel lot.

"That boy that tried to take you."

"What?"

"The pretty one. He just got his face cut."

"What?"

"The gorilla pimp," Coy Hawkins says.

Angel flips to Nikki. Her mouth is dropped. Her hair is messy. She flips back to Coy Hawkins.

"What about that guy last week bashed my head against the wall? He tried to kill me."

Coy Hawkins merges onto the interstate and says nothing.

"Hello?"

Angel looks at Nikki again.

"He wasn't acting like this before you showed up."

Nikki says nothing, too.

"You lost my shoe?"

Nikki looks at her feet. She kicks off the high heel that's left.

THE DAWN IS FOGGY. It shrouds everything in damp white cotton. It makes this place look sweet and fat. Like nothing bad ever happens. Out of the pickup window Nikki watches the bottom road roll by, lying.

"HOW MUCH THOSE MEN PAY YOU?"

Angel is awake. She's balled herself up but Nikki can hear her teeth grind. It's a while before Angel says something.

"Depends," Angel says.

"On what?"

"On what they want."

"What if they want everything?"

"No condom?"

Nikki stares at NO SIGNAL on the TV.

"No condom."

"Two hundred."

"The gorilla pimp offered ten grand for me," Nikki says.

On the couch Angel looks over her shoulder.

NIKKI LOOKS AT ANGEL'S HAND. It's on one of her skinned knees. She takes Angel's hand and moves it to her bikini bottom. Angel looks at Nikki in the mirror. She puts down the eyeliner.

Angel slides her hand under the bikini bottom's elastic. She sticks a finger into Nikki. She pulls it out. She starts to rub Nikki in a circle. In the mirrored closet Angel looks calm and Nikki looks alarmed.

Nikki sits very still. Then she reaches back and pulls Angel by the hair.

Oh, Nikki thinks.

Angel wipes her fingers on a tissue. She chins at the bed.

"Can you tell him to take me to the Super 8 tonight?"

COY HAWKINS GLANCES BACK.

"I don't need you," he says.

Nikki stops dead on the steps. Angel turns back, too, and her face is nasty like it's Nikki's fault. They both get in the pickup and peel off.

She looks across the yard. Levi's just sitting there on his bike.

"What?" Nikki says.

She slams the door behind her.

ALL NIGHT SHE SITS ON THE COUCH in the dark with her mind racing.

He does need her. He couldn't have gotten into that apartment without her, for one thing.

She pictures the black girls, with their mouths wide open, but she doesn't hear them scream.

Back then Coy Hawkins was the biggest coke dealer in the county and now he's not even a gorilla pimp. *Cletus*, she thinks.

She smokes a bunch of Kool Kings in a row and doesn't get sick. She listens to everything.

When the front door squeals open light shoots in. Angel starts to sit on the couch. But she goes around to the other side of the coffee table instead. Angel drops down on the floor. Coy Hawkins sits in his chair.

Nikki looks at him.

"You should have more girls," Nikki says.

Coy Hawkins snaps his fingers at her.

"Put that knife back in the kitchen."

"RENEE," Nikki says.

Nikki slouches in the seat. Renee is sitting on the clinic sidewalk waiting for the group-home van. Renee has physical therapy every Tuesday and Thursday and the van is always late.

"Renee."

Finally Nikki honks. Renee flicks her head and Nikki raises hers above the windowsill. Renee squints. She stands up. She wanders across the parking lot. Already she is taking forever. Nikki rolls her eyes.

When Renee puts her hands on the windowsill she grins.

"Whose car is this?"

"Mine," Nikki says.

Nikki shrugs. Renee smirks.

"Nikki," she says.

"What?"

"You ain't old enough to drive."

Nikki looks at her.

"You wanna go for a ride or what?"

Renee glances at the road.

"All right," she says.

Nikki slumps all through town but they never pass the van.

On the north highway Renee lets her right hand dip through the air. Her right wrist is bulky in a brace. Out of the corner of her eye Nikki watches her. She thinks Renee is prettier than

Angel but not as pretty as her. Renee's hair is blue, but only the underneath part.

She's annoyed that Renee hasn't asked where they're going.

"We're going to my daddy's."

"All right," Renee says.

Nikki turns up the stereo until the whole car is rattling.

Up the hill Levi's in the way again. He's wearing a T-shirt over where she threw the brick at him. She lays on the horn and he jerks his bike to the side.

"Who was that?"

Renee peers out the back window.

"Nobody," Nikki says.

Nikki almost loses control around the last bend. She parks next to the pickup in the yard.

"Damn, your daddy stay out in the boonies."

Nikki looks out at the vacant houses and the tall grass.

"He's got ecstasy."

Renee looks at Nikki.

"Molly?" Renee says.

Nikki reaches into the cup holder. She pulls out the eyeliner.

"Want me to do you?" Nikki says.

Under Renee's eyes there are the thinnest bones. Nikki's hand shakes. She stares at Renee's closed lids even after she's done with her scalp prickling.

The cat's eyes come out crooked.

"You look pretty," Nikki says.

Renee grins. She touches one of Nikki's leopard spots.

"Where'd you get that dress?" she says.

"They're still looking for me, ain't they?"

"Who?" Renee says.

"DSS," Nikki says.

Renee shrugs.

"I guess."

Nikki makes a face. She takes the lipstick from the cup holder. She twists it out.

"You know my daddy's Coy Hawkins."

"Who?" Renee says.

Renee doesn't know anything. Nikki hands the lipstick to her.

"Pull your finger through your teeth."

Coy Hawkins and Angel are both in the living room. They turn from the TV at the same time.

"Angel?" Renee says.

"What's she doing up here?" Angel says.

Nikki leads her to Coy Hawkins's chair.

"This is Renee," she says.

Coy Hawkins just looks at them.

"She's a virgin," Nikki says.

THIS TIME THEY SNORT THE ECSTASY and Coy Hawkins himself passes Nikki the rolled bill.

"INDIAN," Renee says.

Coy Hawkins flips the top card off the deck and it's black. It's the three of clubs.

"Drink," Coy Hawkins says.

Renee chugs her beer.

"Indian," Renee says.

Coy Hawkins turns over the next card and it's black again.

"Drink," Coy Hawkins says.

Beer runs down Renee's chin.

"Indian."

"God, she just don't wanna say nigger," Angel says.

Renee giggles. The next card's red, the nine of diamonds.

"My turn," Renee says.

Coy Hawkins slides the deck in front of her.

"Nigger," Coy Hawkins says.

Angel picks up the deck and throws it at Renee and cards fly everywhere.

"Jesus Christ," Renee says.

Coy Hawkins looks at Angel.

"What, you don't wanna play nigger-Indian?" he says.

They're all sitting at the card table. Nikki feels fucked up.

NIKKI AND RENEE DANCE in the living room. In the yard the pickup doors are open and the stereo is cranked up.

Angel sits on the couch with her arms crossed over her chest. Coy Hawkins sits in his chair with his boots up on his footrest. Angel is not wearing one of her dresses or any makeup.

Renee does a lot of different dances. She does the running man and the cabbage patch. She does the robot. She bends over and pops her ass in the air.

In his chair Coy Hawkins laughs. Nikki grins at him and something warm inside her brain bursts and bursts and bursts.

Angel is watching her.

RENEE MAKES NIKKI go to the bathroom with her.

"You were always so quiet."

Renee's peeing.

"What?" Nikki says.

"I never would've thought."

Renee pulls her shorts up.

"What are you talking about?" Nikki says.

While Renee washes her hands she looks at herself in the mirror. Her red lips smile. She doesn't seem to notice her crooked eyes. Nikki is leaning against the sink, too, but the other way. She also stares at Renee's face.

"Your daddy's handsome."

The ecstasy drips down the back of Nikki's throat.

NIKKI NEARLY BURNS RENEE. Renee's face was far away and then suddenly it was so close. She jerks her cigarette back.

Renee is leaning forward. She is sitting on the arm of Coy Hawkins's chair. Nikki is sitting on the arm of the couch. Renee is looking at Angel, whose arms are still crossed.

"What happened to your glasses?" Renee says.

"What happened to your hand?" Angel says.

Renee covers her wrist brace with her fingers.

"It's been broke," Renee says.

"Her daddy broke it," Nikki says.

Renee looks at Nikki and her cheeks flame up, like when Nikki told she was a virgin, but when she speaks her voice is a long flat line. They all sound that way.

"Nikki," she says.

Coy Hawkins reaches around to stub his cigarette out and then he keeps his hand there, on Renee's hip.

NIKKI FOLLOWS COY HAWKINS into the kitchen. She stands by the card table while he pulls beers from the fridge.

"Virgins make more money," she says.

Coy Hawkins looks at her.

"Don't they?"

He picks up a card from the floor and puts it on the table.

"Drink," he says.

NIKKI SITS NEXT TO ANGEL on the couch. First Coy Hawkins went down the hall and then Renee did. Nikki's waiting for them to come back. She's holding a beer but she hasn't cracked it. Its condensation is all over her leg.

"That gorilla pimp's gonna find me," Angel says.

Nikki looks at her. Angel has her knees up under Coy Hawkins's shirt.

"You seen what he does to their necks?" Angel says.

She touches her throat.

"Every time you look in the mirror you gotta see that shit, even when you're eighty."

"He's so little. How does he even beat them?"

"You don't know nothing," Angel says.

Nikki is looking at the hall again.

"Nikki?"

Her temples are crawling.

Angel's hand slips between Nikki's thighs. Angel's finger drags up the middle of Nikki's bikini bottom. It starts to fuzz, the hallway.

Nikki shoves Angel's hand away.

"What are you doing?" Nikki says.

IN THE BATHROOM MIRROR Nikki is doing something weird, distorted, with her mouth.

THE BATHROOM DOOR SLAPS OPEN.

"I wanna go," Renee says.

Nikki looks at her. Renee's hair's a mess. The skin all around her mouth is red.

"Why?" Nikki says.

Also one of her bra straps is hanging out of her tank top.

"I wanna go right now."

"Did he say you could?" Nikki says.

"What?" Renee says.

Like she even needs a bra. Nikki's sitting on the floor between the toilet and the shower with a towel wrapped around her and Renee's hovering above her.

The rest of Renee's face is white, pale. Nikki doesn't know what she's so upset about.

"Did you know my mama died?" Nikki says.

"What?"

Renee stares at her.

"She jumped off a cliff."

Nikki pulls the towel up to her chin. She's shivering.

Renee's crooked eyes go everywhere, to the electric shaver and the shower curtain and the window that is little and high.

"The law's gonna be looking for me," she says.

Nikki shrugs.

"I guess."

For a second Renee's nose bunches up like she might cry. Then she puts her hands on her hips.

"I gotta puke," Renee says.

She runs into the hall.

"You should puke in the bathroom. Renee."

After a second Nikki pulls herself up.

"God," she says.

NIKKI WATCHES RENEE fly across the yard into the dark. She watches from the trailer's top step.

She feels him behind her. She turns and looks at him.

"Well, go fucking catch her," Coy Hawkins says.

"RENEE," Nikki says.

Luckily the moon is huge. Luckily Renee's tank top is white. Nikki chases after her, dodging old toilets and mattresses and bricks.

"Renee."

The yard shoots up to their waists. The woods are a black wall. Renee doesn't even flinch.

"Renee."

Nikki plunges in, too. She gets tangled in brush. Giant weeds attack her. And then it's so steep they're crawling on their hands and knees. Nikki scrambles behind Renee's feet.

All of a sudden the trees break. The moon shines back. They stand up on a crop of rock. This is the very top of the hill. They just came up the deer cut, Nikki thinks.

Above her Renee turns around.

"Where are you going?" Nikki yells.

Renee puts her hands on her knees.

"He raped me."

Nikki looks over her shoulder at Coy Hawkins.

"He raped me."

Renee's voice bounces off all the smaller hills, rolling away on every side, the darkest things and shimmering.

"He raped me."

Coy Hawkins pulls the gun from his boot and shoots Renee in the face.

RENEE LIES ON A ROCK LEDGE below, her face a hole.

"The old woodpile in the yard, go pull the ax out. There's trash bags in the kitchen," Coy Hawkins says.

He sounds far off though he's standing right in front of her. He has a flashlight. He throws it at Nikki.

In shock she skids down the deer cut.

The woodpile is around the side of the big house with the ax still stuck in it.

"Did you catch her?"

Nikki looks at Angel. She is just standing in the yard with her eyes like saucers. The ax is rusted and Nikki has to brace her foot against the log. With both hands she has to yank the handle.

"Yeah," Nikki says.

Angel backs toward the trailer.

COY HAWKINS is nowhere. She opens her mouth to call him and thinks she doesn't know what to say.

"Hey," Nikki says.

"Down here," Coy Hawkins says.

Coy Hawkins is down on the ledge, squatting by Renee. He squints in the flashlight and points at the path.

The deer cut makes a sudden switch left and leads down the other side of the hill. Nikki has to stoop because this is not a trail made by humans. She is afraid she is going to fall into nothingness. By the time she reaches him she is sweating.

Coy Hawkins stands up.

"Grab my waist. We gotta pull her off this," Coy Hawkins says.

He is skinny when Nikki loops her arms around him. He grips Renee by the shins.

"One, two, three," he says.

They drag her off the ledge and onto the deer cut.

She looks freakish without a face. She no longer looks like a person. With his knife Coy Hawkins strips off her clothes. He cuts off her panties with one flick. She's not shaved. She's peach-fuzzed.

Nikki takes her wrist brace from him. It reveals a weird tan line, a block of white skin. In the flashlight it's almost translucent.

"Did you rape her?" Nikki says.

"What do you think?" Coy Hawkins says.

He slices the pads off each of Renee's fingertips.

"Ax," Coy Hawkins says.

Coy Hawkins jams the butt into what's left of Renee's mouth. Then he raises the ax above his head and brings it down hard on Renee's neck. Nikki bangs into the tree behind her.

"Fingerprints and teeth."

She stares at him.

"Nikki."

"What?"

"You're shaking like a leaf."

"No, I ain't."

"Trash bags," Coy Hawkins says.

After they've finished she looks at the blood on the ground.

"It'll rain," Coy Hawkins says.

Coy Hawkins carries the heavy bags. Nikki follows with the light ones. She waits for him to look where the money's buried. But he doesn't once turn his head.

"Are you mad?" she says.

Wesley's car is gone from the yard. Coy Hawkins looks at the place where it was. Then he goes to the pickup. He flips back the tarp and hefts the heavy bags up into the bed.

"Where's Angel?" Nikki says.

"Throw her clothes on the trash pile," Coy Hawkins says.

Near the other trailer Nikki thinks she sees Levi, sitting on his bike in his pajamas.

THE NORTHERNMOST PART OF THE COUNTY is wilderness. It's a state park that straddles the county line. It has trails that end in sheer drops. It's had fugitives hiding in it. Hunters get lost in here all the time.

The pickup jerks from the gravel road to grass and then a dirt path. They climb at ninety degrees. Branches slap the windows. Coy Hawkins pulls the emergency brake and Nikki slams against the bench seat.

It's dawn now.

"We gotta hike this last little bit," Coy Hawkins says.

He throws the bags out of the bed.

It is so much heavier going up. The light bags thud against Nikki's legs. They're hiking forever. Finally Coy Hawkins crouches below a boulder and Nikki takes huge gulps of air.

He takes out his knife and slashes all the bags of Renee.

"So the animals will eat her."

Nikki grabs the laces of Coy Hawkins's boot.

"Please don't call DSS on me. I can't go back there."

He looks at her fingers. Coy Hawkins wipes his face on his sleeve.

"You ain't going back there now," he says.

He holds on to a trunk to stand up. He tosses a bag over the boulder. He reaches back until all five bags are gone and then he shakes his hand like Nikki has forgotten one.

"Come here," he says.

Nikki looks at him.

"Come here," he says.

He pulls her up to stand beside him.

"Look at this."

Nikki looks where Renee went. She didn't realize they were this high. It is like she could touch the blue mountains. Blue froths everything. Blue fog puffs from the gorge below.

"The Blue Ridge Parkway," Coy Hawkins says.

He points off in the distance at a floating road. Up here the air is like cigarette smoke.

She has the weird feeling he's going to push her. He's still holding her by the arm.

"Can we go?" Nikki says.

"What kind of daughter does that?" Coy Hawkins says.

"Does what?"

"Brings her father a whore."

SHE TRIES TO HIDE what she's doing.

"You seen that lighter?" Nikki says.

She hunts from one end of the trailer to the other. Eventually she comes to stand in front of the TV.

"She'll probably come back," Nikki says.

"Who?" Coy Hawkins says.

NO SIGNAL. Nikki stares at it.

When she looks at Coy Hawkins he's turned in his chair to face her. He has his arm propped up on his elbow. He has his chin in his hand.

"What?" Nikki says.

"You wanna rob a drug dealer?"

THREE

COY HAWKINS stands behind Nikki with his arms laid over her arms, his hands cupping her hands, his fingers on top of her fingers. As they pull the trigger he rams his shoulder into her shoulder.

"Don't flinch."

He walks over to Levi. He picks up his beer and points with it.

"Go ahead," Coy Hawkins says.

Nikki raises the gun at the big house again.

SHE WATCHES HIM push a brush through the barrel. She watches him drop oil on a rag and shine the black metal. The parts fit back together in hard snaps and the magazine clicks in last. He wipes his hands on a rag.

"The first time's the worst," Coy Hawkins says.

"I done it before," Nikki says.

He cuts his eyes to her.

"Wesley Harrell," she says.

Coy Hawkins points his clean gun at one of the walls of the kitchen.

"Oh yeah," he says.

SHE LOOKS AT HIM. She is startled by the bandanna around his face. A second ago he wasn't wearing it. He pulls up his hood. He nods at her.

She knocks on an apartment door, the welfare apartments in town that are gray and wooden and drop down to the riverbank.

When the peephole darkens she takes one step back. The door catches on its chain.

"Hey," Nikki says.

A man stares at her.

"Who are you?"

"Nikki," she says.

"Who?"

"Can I use your phone?"

"What?" he says.

Nikki holds up Coy Hawkins's cell.

"Mine's dead."

The man's eyes flick up and down. Nikki smiles at him. She's wearing a dress with see-through parts. Her cat's eyes are slightly crooked but her lips are very red. When Angel left she left everything.

Nikki jams her knee inside and touches his. He's older than Coy Hawkins. His cheeks are cut by two deep lines.

"Hold up," he says.

As soon as he slams the door Nikki takes two steps back, and when he opens it again, wide, unchained, Coy Hawkins pivots off the outside wall and slugs a baseball bat into the man's gut.

"What the fuck," the man grunts.

She crawls underneath him while Coy Hawkins smashes him over the back.

No one's in the living room. She turns a right for the kitchen like Coy Hawkins said. The other man, the important one, is sitting at a table. His name is Lee Church. He is nothing like she pictured him. She raises the gun and surges at him.

"Drugs and cash," Nikki says.

He looks surprised.

"Drugs and cash."

He just sits there. She starts to panic. She hears Coy Hawkins's bat behind her. She stomps her high heel on the linoleum and lets out a little shriek.

"Are you stupid? This is a motherfucking stickup."

Lee Church puts his cigarette in an ashtray and then he puts his hands up.

THEY'RE PULLED OFF IN THE WOODS, out in the county. Coy Hawkins has a Ziploc bag of cocaine in his lap. Nikki has rubber-banded bills between her feet. That went well, Nikki thinks.

"Don't use your real name next time," Coy Hawkins says.

"Why not?" Nikki says.

He dips the pickup key in the Ziploc. He looks at her. In the overhead light his face is like wax.

"Bump?" he says.

COKE SMELLS COLD AND CHEMICAL like the inside of a refrigerator. It's what back then smells like, now when she thinks of it. Nikki takes a drag off Coy Hawkins's Kool and its blast of menthol is the best thing that's ever been in her mouth.

The interstate reels out. The sign says thirty miles to Charlotte. Coy Hawkins has called somebody on his phone. It's not really dead. This time he's going to sell, Nikki thinks. She is giddy and she can't feel her teeth.

They have already passed over the service road. They have already passed over the gorilla pimp. They could be going anywhere.

SHE LOOKS AROUND ALERTLY. She sniffs drip up her nose.

"Where are we?" Nikki says.

"Kannapolis," Coy Hawkins says.

"Where?"

On both sides of a wide street every house is the same. They glow up in the headlights of the pickup, white and sagging. After a while Coy Hawkins stops in front of one.

A Mexican man opens the door.

"Where the fuck you been?" he says.

Coy Hawkins shrugs.

"Trying to stay out of trouble, man."

Nikki follows him in. The house's living room is strewn with little girls' toys. There's a blow-up castle in the middle of it. Coy Hawkins and the man go into what must be the kitchen. They close a bed sheet behind them.

"You can't go in there."

Nikki looks at her. The little girl is curled on the couch, holding a baby doll and wearing a tutu. She is five or six. Nikki puts her hands on her hips.

"Why not?"

"You're not supposed to," the little girl says.

"Why?" Nikki says.

"Because you're a girl."

"What?"

Nikki thinks she sees the little girl smirk.

"My mom can't even go in there," the little girl says.

Her tutu is much pinker than Nikki's hair used to be. Nikki kicks a Barbie Corvette out of the way of her feet.

"Hey," the little girl says.

Nikki sits beside her.

"My mama's dead," Nikki says.

The little girl makes a face.

"She killed herself," Nikki says.

The little girl drops her mouth on the doll's head.

It's probably four in the morning. They watch TV. It's a flat screen with all the channels. Nikki doesn't understand because it's in Spanish.

"She left me when I was a baby," Nikki says.

She doesn't know why she just said that. She smells something like burning ketchup.

"You smell that?"

The little girl says nothing. Nikki looks at the bed sheet.

"What is it?"

"Papi," the little girl says.

Nikki stands up and the girl cuts her eyes from the TV. For a second they stare at each other. The little girl is not going to be as pretty as her. If she touched the little girl she would be gooey, Nikki thinks. Nikki sits down again.

When the bed sheet opens Coy Hawkins is carrying a different grocery bag than the one he came in with. He snaps his fingers at Nikki.

"My daughter," Coy Hawkins says.

The man looks at her briefly.

"HOW MUCH DID YOU GET FOR IT?"

"Half a ki of heroin," Coy Hawkins says.

Nikki's eyes dart to the bag between her feet.

"What?"

On the way home they stop and buy party balloons.

THE HEROIN IS BLACK. It's sticky. It's shiny.

"What's wrong with it?"

"Nothing," Coy Hawkins says.

They're in the kitchen. They're sitting at the card table. Coy Hawkins has ripped open the bag of party balloons.

"It ain't white," Nikki says.

"It's black tar."

"It's what?"

"Mexican shit," Coy Hawkins says.

He breaks off a tarry black chunk.

"You got everybody up here snorting pills and paying what?"

Nikki shrugs. Coy Hawkins answers his own question.

"A dollar a milligram. Eighty dollars for one fucking eighty," he says.

He nudges the black chunk onto a balloon's head. He turns the balloon inside out, knots it, pushes it through so that it's right side out, and knots it again. He holds it up.

"How much you think this costs?"

"I don't know," Nikki says.

"Ten dollars."

"What?"

He clips it to a scale and hangs it before him.

"Tenth of a gram," he says.

He tosses it to her.

"Whoever brings this shit up here first is gonna make a killing."

Nikki just stares at him.

"I'm trying to teach you something," Coy Hawkins says.

She is not paying attention. She is thinking about how much better it would be if the table were covered in cash. She looks at the black lump. It doesn't even seem like that much. Her jaw is still going from that one bump.

"Pills are the same as heroin?"

Coy Hawkins laughs.

"Yeah," he says.

The balloon is blue. It's tiny. Nikki looks at it again.

SHE YAWNS. When she stumbles into the kitchen a man and a woman are sitting there. They turn to her. Then they turn to Coy Hawkins.

"It's cool," he says.

He has a roll of tinfoil.

He tears off a sheet. He quarters it and rips it into squares. He burns the side of one piece with his lighter. He sticks heroin to the other side. He wraps another square around a pen and pushes it out and makes a straw.

He holds up the heroin foil. He flicks his lighter under it. There is a long crackling as he pulls up smoke. He lifts his head with the straw between his lips. He blows out and the whole kitchen explodes in burning ketchup.

Nikki leans against a wall.

Coy Hawkins fixes a second foil and passes it to the woman.

"See how it slides. Chase it," he says.

The woman waves her hand.

"I smoked Oxys before," she says.

"That's the stupidest thing I ever heard," Coy Hawkins says.

She looks insulted but when Coy Hawkins flicks the lighter she lowers her head.

The man peers over the woman's shoulder. When the woman has a coughing fit the man takes the foil from her and lights it for himself.

"Shooting's better," Coy Hawkins says.

He shivers.

"You get that rush."

The woman shakes her head.

"I don't fuck with needles."

"You'll get over it," Coy Hawkins says.

"How much?" the man says.

Coy Hawkins throws out a handful of balloons.

"Tell your friends," he says.

The man is picking up the balloons that fell on the floor. He's stuffing his socks with them. Nikki feels light. She watches the burnt-ketchup smoke settle onto everything, onto a missed patch of hair on the man's shaved head.

Nikki drops her foot on a yellow one. She curls her toes over it. The man looks at her. He narrows his eyes. She glares back at him.

"What?" she says.

The man scratches his leg. He sits up.

"Fucking Coy Hawkins. In the flesh," he says.

NIKKI SITS on the bathroom floor to concentrate. Smoking heroin's harder than it looks.

She burns herself. Her mouth fills with bitter, vinegary smoke and she coughs. The heroin slides in a brown streak over the lit foil and she chases it. Finally it stops rolling. It blackens and pops.

She leans against the shower with the straw in her mouth. She feels nothing.

SHE PUKES IN THE TOILET.

NIKKI WANDERS into the kitchen. There are different men and women. She's never seen them before.

She wants something to kill the taste in her mouth. She stands in the open refrigerator staring. A man asks her something and before she can answer asks her something else.

"What?" Nikki says.

She feels a pinch on her arm and after she turns around she sees Coy Hawkins. She looks at him like she would anyone. She doesn't even care.

"You seen that other roll of tinfoil?" he says.

"What?" Nikki says.

She is made of air.

"Go sit on the couch," Coy Hawkins says.

On the couch Nikki scratches up and down her shins. She scratches her arms. She scratches her neck. She scratches especially behind her knees, the backs of her hands just brushing the plaid of the cushions, and murmurs to herself.

She's itchy like she's been snorting pills but heroin is a real drug. Real drugs are a secret. Nikki has always loved secrets. Back then was full of them.

Nikki blinks at the TV. She sees her palms open in her lap. Bewildered she looks all around the living room but there's no one there.

Her head droops again. Her eyes close. It's okay, she thinks, everything.

ON HEROIN SHE DREAMS. She dreams a wild dream she can't control. Mostly a mutant tries to eat her. Nikki snaps awake.

IN THE KITCHEN Coy Hawkins is talking to a man. Nikki stands there a second.

"Plus it's more cost-effective, shooting it," Coy Hawkins says.

"We're gonna make a killing," Nikki says.

They both look at her.

"What?" Coy Hawkins says.

"Us."

Nikki says this only to him. Coy Hawkins puts his fingers up to his lips.

"We're gonna bring this shit up here first and it's gonna be like back then. You're gonna be the biggest in the county again."

Coy Hawkins stares at her. Then he drops his hand from his mouth and starts laughing. The man looks at Coy Hawkins. He starts laughing, too.

NIKKI WASHES HER HAIR. She shaves everywhere. She brushes her teeth and spits out blood in the sink. She stares at a bleached blonde hair. She blasts the faucet until it gets sucked down the drain.

She opens the cabinet underneath. She pulls out the hair dryer and flat iron and the whole pouch of makeup.

She looks at her face in the mirror. She does not see a stupid little girl.

SHE HAS TO WALK almost all the way down to the bottom road before she gets reception on Coy Hawkins's phone.

"its nikki. hey," she texts.

She drops the grocery bag between her feet. She keeps looking over her shoulder. She glares at Levi, a few hundred feet above her. The phone lights up.

"what," Wesley texts.

"i wanna see u," Nikki texts.

"why"

"??" Wesley texts.

Nikki rolls her eyes.

"just come get me im at my dads," she texts.

"Go tell your grandmama I'm waiting on a ride. Ain't that who you're spying for?" Nikki says.

Levi makes a face like he can't hear and then he pedals up the hill.

"u owe me," Wesley texts.

WESLEY LOCKS AND CHAINS the camper door. It's just the two of them. Nikki peeks around the curtain at the air mattress to make sure.

"Where's old girl?" Nikki says.

"What do you want?" Wesley says.

Her hair is huge. She's wearing the best of the dresses and she's brought balloons. When she dumps out the grocery bag onto Wesley's table ten or so tumble out.

Wesley comes close to her. He chins at the table without breaking his stare.

"What the fuck is that?"

"Black tar heroin," Nikki says.

He grabs her by the back of the neck. He slams her forehead to her knees.

"Quit it," she shrieks.

"You wearing a fucking wire?"

"No, get off me."

"Where the fuck you get it?"

"From my daddy, where you think?"

Wesley pulls his hand out of her dress. He lets go and she shoves him in the chest.

"Asshole," Nikki says.

She slouches back on the couch. Wesley sits down beside her and picks up a balloon. He weighs it in his palm.

"It's the same as pills."

"Yeah, I know," Wesley says.

"Except it's way cheaper and better," Nikki says.

"You done it?"

Nikki kicks under the table at the bag of Mama's clothes.

"Yeah," she says.

Wesley gets up. He steps around the table. They're already in the kitchen. He opens some drawers. He steps back with a roll of tinfoil.

"Right?" he says.

"It's better if you shoot it," Nikki says.

She shivers.

"You get that rush."

Wesley kind of laughs. He sits down and opens the balloon with his teeth. He tears off a piece of foil and smudges the heroin onto it and it gleams.

"No," Nikki says.

"What?" Wesley says.

"You're doing it wrong."

"I'm doing it wrong?"

"You gotta burn off the shiny side."

"Why?"

"Because."

Nikki sighs. She unfolds her arms and takes the foil from him.

"You gotta pen?" she says.

She shows him.

She makes a straw. She fixes a foil and lights it. As the heroin rolls she chases it. She lifts her head with smoke in her mouth and Wesley's eyes glint.

"What?"

Wesley shakes his head.

"Nothing," he says.

She makes one for him. She stares at his bent head while he smokes it. Like this is hard, Nikki thinks.

"You heard about Lee Church?" Nikki says.

"What?"

Wesley's coughing.

"Lee Church. He stays in them Glenhaven apartments."

Wesley blows burnt-ketchup smoke out of the side of his mouth.

"I heard he got robbed."

Nikki gathers all her hair to one side. She pulls her fingers through it and tilts her head and looks at him.

"By a couple Mexicans," Wesley says.

"Mexicans?"

He's looking at the foil straw.

"No, it wasn't," Nikki says.

"I heard it from Lee Church himself. The fucking cartel," Wesley says.

THERE ARE THREE OR FOUR STRANGE CARS in the yard.

On the couch there are strange people nodding out.

"Where the fuck you been?"

Coy Hawkins leans out of the kitchen.

"Like you care," Nikki says.

She goes down the hall. She slams the bathroom door as hard as she can.

LATER SHE SEES HIM go into the bedroom. She goes after him. His hair is wet and in the mirrored closet he's combing it. Nikki sits on the bed, watching him.

"Lee Church is telling everybody it was two Mexicans that robbed him," she says.

"So what?" Coy Hawkins says.

"So why would he say that?"

In the mirror Coy Hawkins's eyes shift to her.

"Why do you think?" Coy Hawkins says.

Behind him Nikki looks at herself. Then she looks at the green carpet. It's so ugly, she thinks. She shoves her toes into it. She crosses her arms over her chest.

"You think I'm just bait," she says.

"No," he says.

He turns around and looks at her. He grips the towel around his waist by its knot. She stares at Mama's name on him. It's almost gone, too. He throws his comb on the bed and holds his hand out.

"Give me my phone back," he says.

Later still a man walks in on her in the bathroom. She rips her dress down but he just stands there. She doesn't know what to do. She nearly hisses at him.

"Get out," Nikki says.

The man leans against the wall on one hand.

"Calm down," he says.

She wiggles out under his arm.

"IS THERE A NIKKI HERE?" a woman says.

From the couch Nikki glares.

"Yeah. What?" she says.

The woman starts scratching her arm. She closes her eyes.

"Some guy's looking for you," the woman says.

In the yard is Wesley. Nikki freezes on the trailer's top step. She thinks about calling Coy Hawkins. But Wesley's alone this time. He is looking around at the other cars.

"What happened to my ride?" Wesley says.

Luckily she hasn't changed. The best of the dresses laces up the sides.

"We didn't want it no more," she says.

She reties two bows.

"What are you doing up here?"

Wesley puts his hands in his pockets and shrugs.

"I wanna buy an ounce," he says.

Nikki tries to hide her grin but can't. She opens the trailer door and looks over her shoulder.

She kicks everybody out of the kitchen. Then she shuts the accordion door. She grabs a beer from the refrigerator and cracks it and sets it on the card table in front of him.

Wesley tilts back in his chair and crosses his arms behind his head.

"Where's Coy Hawkins?" he says.

"Why?" Nikki says.

He looks at her. She puts her hands on her hips.

"Just one, right?" she says.

Wesley laughs. He lets his chair bang the floor. He takes the cigarette from behind his ear and sticks it in his mouth.

"Wait here," Nikki says.

She goes into the bedroom where the bigger chunks are stashed. They're stuffed in the toes of Coy Hawkins's boots and wrapped in cut-up grocery bags. She pulls one out. Coy Hawkins is lying on the bed.

"What are you doing?" he says.

"Selling an ounce to Wesley Harrell."

She nearly bounces back to the kitchen. She closes the accordion door behind her. She tosses the chunk on the card table.

"One piece," Nikki says.

Wesley stubs his cigarette out.

"That's what you call heroin ounces," she says.

"Okay," he says.

He has his own scale. He pulls it out like a gun. Nikki perches on the chair across from him. She puts her face in her hand.

He takes the chunk off the scale.

"It's short," he says.

He puts it on again.

"It's twenty-five."

"I know," Nikki says.

Wesley looks at her.

"There's twenty-eight grams in an ounce," he says.

"It's heroin weight."

"What?"

"It's a Mexican ounce," Nikki says.

"A what?"

Nikki racks her brain for all the other things Coy Hawkins has said.

"It's the metric system, dumb ass," Coy Hawkins says.

Nikki flicks her head. He's standing with one arm folding open the accordion door. After a second Wesley nods at him.

"Makes sense," Wesley says.

He reaches in his pocket and then he looks at Coy Hawkins. "How much, man?" he says.

Wesley's beer is still where Nikki put it. She picks it up and hurls it at the wall.

SHE STALKS DOWN THE HALL. In the bedroom she bangs the door behind them. Coy Hawkins goes over to the bed and sits on it. He looks up at her.

"That's my money," she says.

He counts out half the twenties and pushes them across the mattress.

"You need to be careful," he says.

"Of what?" Nikki says.

Coy Hawkins shakes his head. He snaps toward the kitchen.

"Go clean up that mess."

NIKKI TUCKS THE STRAW behind her ear. She smiles at herself. Her pupils are the tiny heads of pins. Her eyes are the bluest blue. She reaches up and rests her arms on top of her head and she can count all her ribs in the bathroom mirror.

She thinks she looks great. But her hair is brownish again. Under the sink is a bleach kit.

When she comes out the trailer's dark. She wants to show someone. She finds him in the living room. He's stretched out in his chair. She turns on the floor lamp and grins.

"You like it?" Nikki says.

Coy Hawkins squints at her. He feels for his cigarettes.

"Not really," he says.

THERE IS A MAN WITH A NEEDLE. Nikki watches him.

He pushes the black tar out of a balloon and into a bottle cap. He adds a splash of water and burns his lighter underneath. The bottle cap is metal. The heroin starts to bubble.

He pulls the head off a Q-tip. He drops the cotton in the cap and pushes it around with the needle tip. He pulls the plunger up with his teeth.

He has a rubber tie like a nurse. He yanks it around the woman's arm. Big green veins stand up when he slaps her. He rubs his thumb over one.

He jabs the needle in and then he wiggles it some. Blood blooms into the syringe. Slowly he pushes the plunger until all the black-red liquid runs in.

Nikki watches the woman's head fall to her chest and stay there like it's broken. Nikki sits down in the other chair. She puts her arm on the card table.

"Do me," she says.

The man stares at her.

"Ain't this your daddy's place?" he says.

Nikki shrugs.

"So?"

The man takes off his baseball hat and turns it around the other way. He pulls it low over his eyes.

"Shit," he says.

He holds her arm by the wrist and tears opens another balloon. She can see into the living room from her chair and down the hall to the bedroom door. She waits for Coy Hawkins to open it.

The needle pricks going in. After he slides it out Nikki's arm flares with a white-hot itch from shoulder to fingertip.

SHE CAREENS THROUGH THE DARK. She can only see the dashboard before her. She is not driving and she cannot wake up but she knows she is being chased. The road breaks.

HEROIN IS THE MOST SECRET OF THEM ALL and needles are the most secret part and she has always loved secrets ever since she was a little girl.

SHE DREAMS that Coy Hawkins is strangling her. She goes into the bathroom to look at her neck and there is a purple ring around her throat. She is overcome with the feeling that her skin is quivering three inches from the rest of her and if she touched it, it would give like a sponge. It's a fat girl's neck that doesn't belong to her. She has to squat down to keep from puking. A loud noise jerks her up. She is awake. She is sitting in the kitchen chair.

"Damn, she looks like she just got her wings," somebody says.

COY HAWKINS is sitting in the other chair. Where the man used to be. He's looking at her arm. Nikki looks at it, too. There's dried blood in the crook of her elbow.

She blinks at him. She thinks she sees something flicker across his face before he goes back to looking at her like always.

"You're fucking up."

He says this and gets up.

NIKKI FEELS FLUISH. She's wrapped in a blanket. She lies like a dead thing on the couch. The front door squeals. Wesley walks in. He looks at her. He nods at her bleached head.

"Nice," he says.

That other man comes in behind him, the big one from before, the Bubba. He has to stoop. His eyes fly around the living room. Nikki sits up.

"You know Chad?" Wesley says.

"What's up?" Bubba says.

She just stares.

"What do you want?"

Wesley snaps his fingers and clicks his fists together.

"Two pieces," he says.

She stands up. She points at them.

"You have to wait outside," she says.

She locks the door behind them. She hurries into the bedroom. She knocks two chunks out of Coy Hawkins's boots. She searches for him. Of course he is nowhere. In the kitchen she grabs the knife.

She flings the front door wide. They're both leaning against a car. She goes down the steps and through the yard.

"Whoa," Wesley says.

"Goddamn," Bubba says.

They only put up their hands halfway again. The knife's trembling.

"You can't just bring anybody up here."
Nikki shoves the two chunks into Wesley's chest.
"Cash," she says.

"WHERE WERE YOU?"

Onto the card table Coy Hawkins throws the pickup keys.

"Out," he says.

He shrugs. He sits down in the chair across from her. He puts his leg up on his knee. Then he switches it. He's sweaty. When she tries to meet his eye he looks at the ceiling. He stands up.

She watches him walk down the hall, stiffly. She sees his keys.

IT MUST BE SATURDAY NIGHT. In town the cruise line crawls through the Walmart parking lot. It clogs all the aisles. Everybody in every passing car squints into the pickup, trying to see who it is. Nikki rolls her eyes.

When she finally gets inside it's bright and huge like always but now, she thinks, she could buy anything.

First she does everything she's never been allowed to do. She sprays on perfume. She tries on lingerie. She looks at shrimp rings and steaks. In electronics she leans against a display case and watches the wall of TVs for a while.

She buys a phone and minutes for it. She pays with bills peeled off a thick wad.

In the parking lot she passes these girls she knows from middle school sitting on the hood of a car. She looks at them like she's never seen them before. Also she bought a pair of black boots. They have chains and they ring as she goes by.

"SQUARE?" the nail lady says.

Nikki makes a face.

"Pointy," she says.

The nail lady shakes the polish bottle. They're the only ones in here. The nail lady has a paper face mask but Nikki does not. The fumes are suffocating only her.

"I want red instead," Nikki says.

The nail lady puts down the hot pink. She winks at Nikki.

"So grown-up," she says.

Nikki glares at her.

WITH HER NEW NAILS it's hard to open peanut shells. She tosses a few on the floor. She's never had fake tips. She's never been here before. It's not so great. It's full of the same rednecks as everywhere else. She smokes a cigarette. She sits in the corner of a booth and scratches her puncture wound.

"Sweetie, you all right?"

She looks at the ash that's dripped on top of her steak and then up at the waitress.

"What?" Nikki says.

IN THE STEAKHOUSE PARKING LOT she thinks it's them: DSS. They get out of a plain car. They walk right at her. They look like a regular man and woman but Nikki knows she has seen them.

She turns on her heel. She goes back inside. She marches past the hostess. All through the dining room the floor crunches. It's a carpet of shells. She slips out the back door and runs to the woods.

For a long time she crouches up on a hill. She tries not to break a twig. Some cooks come out dragging garbage bags but that's it.

On the way back a car flashes its brights and she freaks out until it swerves around, passing her.

SHE WANTS TO RUN OVER his stupid bike. Levi trails her around the last bend and into the yard. Another car is parked where the pickup goes. She pulls in next to it. She climbs out.

"Don't you have any friends?" she yells at him.

Before she opens the trailer door she stands on her tiptoes. She peers into the window that looks like a fan.

The living room's empty. The man in the kitchen squints at her. He grins. He slaps his hand on the card table.

"Jesus Christ, look at her."

Nikki stands in the kitchen doorway and stares at him.

"You remember me?" he says.

"No," she says.

Yes, she does. His face is mostly teeth.

"Come on. I used to be over at the house all the time."

He chins toward the big house. He's sitting across from Coy Hawkins.

"You took my fucking truck," Coy Hawkins says.

The crack looks like a sugar cookie. It's knotted in a baggie, white and flat. It's on the table by Coy Hawkins's fingers. Nikki nods at it.

"What's that?" she says.

Coy Hawkins takes a long guzzle of his beer before he looks at her again.

Absently Nikki drops the bag in her hands.

"I got you steak," she says.

SHE HATES THE SMELL OF CRACK. It makes her heart race. It makes her nervous. Every five minutes it sneaks its burning-plastic stink under the bathroom door.

Back then she used to sing. She hums to herself. She fumbles with a balloon. She almost rips off her new nails. She can't do anything with them.

Gunshots. Hunters.

"It's okay," she says.

Later she sits in a ring of burnt foil. She looks at her arms and legs. She is so pale, she thinks. Though it's summer still.

HE FUCKS HER UP AGAINST THE DRESSER. She puts her hands out so her head doesn't slam the mirror. Something is rubbing a raw place on her neck. She turns and grabs his ear in her teeth and jerks. He staggers back. Onto the carpet she spits a diamond stud. When she looks at him his face is as pretty as always.

"Didn't my daddy cut you?"

The gorilla pimp shoves a gun in her mouth. That's how he does it. Nikki fights to wake up.

WESLEY'S IN THE YARD.

"Don't shoot," he says.

It's just him. He's grinning. Nikki looks at her hands but she doesn't have a gun or a knife or anything. She sways on the steps. She's really high.

"Can I come in?"

She wonders what her hair looks like. She touches it. Nikki shrugs at him.

They sit at the card table.

"He here?" Wesley says.

Nikki looks down the hall at the shut bedroom door and shakes her head.

"How much you want?" she says.

"A ki," Wesley says.

Nikki thinks about this. She reaches down and scratches her leg.

"A ki?"

"Yeah."

"Who goes from two ounces to a ki?" she says.

"Look, I got the money. If you can get it," Wesley says.

Nikki looks at him.

She picks up the pen on the table. She grabs his arm and stretches it out and writes the number of her new phone on the inside of it.

Wesley's grinning again. The bedroom door opens. Coy

Hawkins comes out. He is butt-naked except for his boots. Nikki watches him walk down the hall and into the kitchen.

He opens the refrigerator. He closes it with a beer in his hand. His dick is not tall and pink. It hangs like a shrimp from a matted tuft of hair. He looks at them.

"Sup?" Wesley says.

Coy Hawkins cracks his beer. Nikki watches him walk back down the hall and into the bedroom and shut the door.

Under the table Wesley kicks her.

"YOU KNOW HOW MUCH A KI COSTS?"

"A lot," Nikki says.

Coy Hawkins looks at her.

"Yeah," he says.

In the kitchen he's opening all the cabinets.

"So what you gotta ask yourself is where is he getting the money?" Coy Hawkins says.

"Where do you think?"

Coy Hawkins looks at her again. His eyes get wide.

"It could be a lot of people," he says.

He opens all the drawers.

"What are you doing?" Nikki says.

"Looking for something."

"Why were you naked before?"

"I was jerking off."

"Oh," she says.

Coy Hawkins is holding a crack pipe. The glass is clouded up. It's already burnt brown. He points it at her.

"That boyfriend of yours is trying to cut us out."

Coy Hawkins walks into the living room.

SHE IS SKINNIER THAN SHE HAS EVER BEEN. Also she is blonder. Naked, in the bathroom mirror, she stares at herself. He's just jealous, she thinks. Because she's moving weight and he's not. She slips a hand between her legs.

SHE SEES HIM IN THE MIRROR. He comes up behind her. He pulls her hair. He pulls until her neck is arched and her head is tilted back.

"I'm the man and you're the girl," Coy Hawkins says.

She wants to say something back but she can't close her mouth. She hates these wild bad dreams. She hears a loud bang. She is awake.

Earlier the man was here and she bought a needle off him for a dollar. Nikki looks at it. It's stuck in her arm.

Bang. Bang. Bang.

WHEN SHE COMES OUT into the living room there's a hole in the wall. It's a small hole but it goes all the way through to pink insulation. Coy Hawkins has turned his chair from the TV to face it. Plaster's rained around him. He stabs his bat in the carpet.

"I'm looking for something," he says.

"What?" Nikki says.

"Cameras."

Coy Hawkins stands up and then he sits down again.

"Probably."

"You're fucking up," Nikki screams.

SHE HOLDS HER PHONE in the air. She walks almost to the bottom road. When she gets reception all her texts come in at once. They're all from the same number. The last one says "u owe me remember."

Nikki leans against a tree. She stares at the woods for a second. They're gloomy and still. They look like they don't give a shit, she thinks.

"i can get it," she texts.

Up above her Levi's zigzagging the hill. Back and forth, lazily. He's not even looking at her. Her phone glows.

"come here," Wesley texts.

The keys are in the pickup where she left them.

"THAT'S THE MONEY?"

"Yeah," Wesley says.

The book bag's on the built-in table. It's unzipped. It's full of cash. Nikki stands in the camper with her hands on her hips.

"Where did you get it?" she says.

"I got a couple investors."

"Investors?"

Wesley mutes the TV. The girls stop groaning. He chins at the couch beside him.

"Sit down," he says.

She perches on the very edge. The curtain's pushed all the way back. It looks picked up in there, like he stuffed all the redneck girl's stuff behind the air mattress.

"This shit's the future," Wesley says.

Nikki looks at him. He's holding a heroin balloon. There's a whole party bag of them and a scale on the table, too.

"I know," Nikki says.

"I know you robbed Lee Church," Wesley says.

She stares at him.

"What?"

Wesley puts his hand on her leg.

"You don't need him."

"Who?" Nikki says.

"Coy Hawkins," Wesley says.

His pupils are so pinned. His greenest green eyes almost sparkle at her. He squeezes her thigh.

"It could be just me and you," he says.

Nikki looks at the book bag. So does Wesley. Then he leans back on the couch.

"Your guy, he's in Charlotte?" Wesley says.

Nikki nods at him.

"You're trying to cut me out."

"What?" Wesley says.

Nikki picks up the glass ashtray. She smashes it as hard as she can over Wesley's head.

Blood pours out. He tries to stand up and his knees buckle.

"You fucking cunt," he says.

Nikki grabs the book bag again. Also the bag of Mama's clothes:

SHE MERGES ONTO THE INTERSTATE and it is jerky and insane. The pickup is much harder to drive than Wesley's car. She has to muscle the steering wheel. She rides the brakes to read the road signs and tractor-trailers wail around.

She takes the Kannapolis exit. It's a long, winding highway and then stop signs and stoplights and finally boxy lots with short grass and chain fences.

She parks on a wide street where every house looks the same. She does not clean off her cat's eyes. In the rearview mirror she just lines over what's left. They are wilder than Angel's. They look much more like wings.

She climbs the steps of a white and sagging house. She takes a deep breath. She closes her eyes and opens them.

The little girl answers the door in her tutu. Nikki smiles at her.

"Is your daddy in?"

THEY WATCH TV. It's in Spanish but by now Nikki understands. She's been here for an hour. She looks at the bed sheet.

The little girl lies on the couch with her feet in the air. She has matching pink slippers. She has a different baby doll. She's chewing on its plastic fist. Nikki looks at her.

Nikki takes the baby doll out of the little girl's mouth. She knocks over the blow-up castle. She cracks the front door and throws the doll out. When she comes back the little girl is sitting up. Nikki waits for her to cry but she screams instead. A high shriek that pierces Nikki's ears.

Nikki shrieks, too, much louder than the little girl until the little girl is silent and staring.

Nikki looks up. The bed sheet is open. The girl's father is standing in the doorway to the kitchen with his arms crossed over his chest.

THERE ARE NO TOYS IN THE KITCHEN. There is a table with a lace cloth and two wooden chairs. The man sits in one and Nikki sits in the other.

"Where's your father?" he says.

"He couldn't come," she says.

"Why not?"

"He's busy."

"So he sent you?"

Nikki shrugs. The man has his chin in his hand. He's studying her. She studies him, too. His face is moonlike. She's holding the book bag in her lap with her arms through the straps.

"What's your father busy doing?"

"Busting holes in our walls with a bat."

The man's eyes laugh.

"I want a ki," Nikki says.

He crosses his legs.

"How old are you?" he says.

"Sixteen," she says.

The man smirks. Nikki shifts in her chair. It creaks.

"I was twelve when I started. But I was a boy."

"Oh," Nikki says.

She tries smiling at him. There is a long silence.

She feels queasy. She cuts her eyes to the bed sheet. She thinks she has fucked up. At the very least he's going to rob her, she thinks.

He tilts his head.

"The element of surprise is a powerful thing."

"What?" Nikki says.

The man stands in his chair. He pushes up a tile and reaches into the ceiling. A black lump of heroin falls onto the lace and Nikki nearly jumps out of her skin.

They keep coming. Some of them thud onto the floor. They keep coming until there are forty of them.

The man climbs down.

"What's your name?" he says.

She stares at him. She thinks about what Coy Hawkins said. "Nikki."

"Nikki, I'm gonna tell you what I tell that crackhead father of yours. If he fucks me I'm gonna fuck you in front of him. Then I'm gonna cut him so his insides fall out. Then I'm gonna cut you so your insides fall out next to him."

The man touches his chest.

"I'm Junior," he says.

Junior leans back in his chair. He rubs his neck.

"Don't speak to my daughter again."

Nikki looks at the table. She chins at the kilo.

"How much?" she says.

SHE HARDLY NOTICES THE INTERSTATE. She happens to glance at the gas gauge and the black arrow's dangling below the red E like it's broken.

"Fuck," Nikki says.

She takes the next exit. As soon as the ramp curves she sees it's the service road.

"Fuck," Nikki says.

It's so bright. She pulls into the first gas station. She walks fast through the lot and looks in every direction. It's a different store and a different register man but still her heart's beating out of her chest.

"What pump?"

"What?" Nikki says.

The man taps his fingers on the counter. Nikki sees her. She's by the coffee machine. Nikki just stares.

"Angel?" Nikki says.

She feels giddy and like she might vomit. The girl tucks her hair behind her ear and her neck screams. The black letters are like a stamp on her pale skin. They look like they're choking her.

"Angel?"

Nikki goes to her. Nikki grabs her arm. But it's not Angel's face that turns to her. It's somebody else's. Nikki lurches from it.

"What?" the girl says.

THERE'S A DEAD RAT hanging from the trailer when she gets back. It's strung up by a foot and tied to the doorknob. It's skinny. It's silky gray. Nikki rips it down.

Levi is not in the yard. He did not escort her up the hill either. She marches to the other trailer and slams the rat against the front door. Its head explodes.

"Levi," Nikki yells.

"Nikki," Coy Hawkins says.

She flips to him. He's standing on their top step. He has their door wide open. He snaps at her.

"Now," he says.

Inside the pink hole is bigger than she remembers. She stands in the middle of the living room staring at it.

"What's that?" Coy Hawkins says.

Nikki's holding a grocery bag. She looks at it.

"A ki," she says.

"A ki."

Coy Hawkins is standing in front of her.

"I went to Junior's," she says.

"Junior's," he says.

"Yeah."

He's really close to her face.

"Junior let you in the kitchen?"

"Yeah."

"And what did you have to do for him?"

Nikki purses her lips. She looks at him. He looks coiled up. He looks cracked out.

"Nothing," she says.

"You got the money from Wesley Harrell?"

Nikki shrugs. She kicks the coffee table and her boot rings.

"He's got investors," she says.

Coy Hawkins is rocking on his feet. He's blocking her from the hallway. She tries to see around him. They're the only ones here.

"Where is everybody?" she says.

"The feds give cash," Coy Hawkins says.

Nikki looks at him.

"What?"

"They buy steak dinners, too," he says.

"What are you talking about?"

"Who else you seen while you were out?"

"Nobody," she says.

"You ain't seen Lee Church?"

He's trembling.

"No."

"You ain't seen my sister?"

"In prison?"

"You ain't seen Robby Greer?"

"Who?"

"What do you mean who? The goddamn sheriff."

Nikki takes a step back.

"Your story's full of holes," Coy Hawkins says.

She shakes her head.

"Everything's there."

Another step.

"You just ain't listening," she says.

He grabs her as soon as she starts to run. She sticks out her hand but he gets her by the hair until all she can see are his eyes, which are the blackest beads. It's happening again, she thinks, wildly.

"You could have got yourself killed."

"Daddy," Nikki says.

Coy Hawkins yanks her arm the wrong way.

FOUR

SHE IS NOT DEAD.

She smells piss when she peels herself off the living room floor. Coy Hawkins is in his chair. He has a fist to his lips and he's jittering his knee up and down.

It takes her a while to get to the door. It takes her forever to cross the yard. On the steps of the other trailer she has to squat down with the grocery bag. She sees rat brains. She pukes between her feet. Levi swings the door out.

"Look at your face," Levi says.

"BILLIE," Nikki says.

Levi's grandmama is in the bedroom. She's on the brass bed under the chintzy comforter. Nikki recognizes that. Nikki does not recognize her.

Her cheeks are hollow. Her hair is messy and white. She looks like an old woman. She's swallowed by throw pillows.

Nikki shoves her.

"Billie."

Her eyes are closed. They're heavy hoods.

"She's sick," Levi says.

Nikki stares at her.

Back down the hall she holds on to the wall. In the living room she sees the stiff couch with the hump in its back. All this furniture is from the big house. Nikki climbs onto it on her knees. She tucks her head in a corner of it. She balls herself up.

THIS TRAILER is a twin to the other one. Except nothing is the same. Here there are fake flowers on fake vines and branches. There are boxes, bowls, and pitchers of potpourri. There are yellow-looking doilies and frog-shaped ashtrays.

The dust sometimes looks like spiderwebs and sometimes looks like lace. It hangs from the ceiling. It trails down the walls.

Nikki reaches out and kicks Levi. He's asleep in one of the stiff chairs that match the stiff couch. He wakes up with a terrified look on his face.

"What?" Levi says.

"Rat," Nikki says.

"What?"

Levi rubs his eyes.

"Rat," Nikki says.

"That wasn't me."

Levi gets up and changes the channel on the TV. It's also rabbit-eared. It's even smaller than Coy Hawkins's.

Nikki tries to get up, too. Her face feels like it's going to separate. She lets her head drop back on the couch.

"Don't ever do that again," she says.

"What?"

She closes her eyes.

"Your grandmama, she don't go out no more?" Nikki says.

"Nope," Levi says.

She looks at him. He's in the chair again. He pulls his knees up to his chest.

"Who brings your food?"

"Some church."

Nikki rolls her eyes.

"They think dinosaurs and men lived at the same time."

"What?" Nikki says.

"They think we rode dinosaurs."

Nikki smirks.

"They do," he says.

Levi grins, too. He stares at her.

"She's got pain pills, don't she?" Nikki says.

Levi shrugs.

"She's got lollipops," he says.

"Do what?"

"Fentanyl or something. You suck on it."

He sniffs the air.

"You stink," he says.

SHE SCOWLS AT HER FACE. One cheek is puffy. One eye is filled with blood. Her lip is split and her nails are ruined.

They're in a box under the sink. They're plastic sticks. They look like tiny barbells and they taste like blueberry.

In the bathroom mirror Nikki shifts the lollipop from the right side of her mouth to the left.

HER SKIN IS LEAD. Her eyelids are tombstones. Her lungs are so slow. Nikki falls asleep in the shower and wakes up freezing. She sees purple mold everywhere. Fuck, Nikki thinks.

SHE CRAWLS UP on the brass bed.

"He did it again," she says.

Billie says nothing.

"He hit me. He fucked up my face."

Billie doesn't answer. In the mirrored closet Nikki sees herself.

"He's my daddy," Nikki says.

She starts to disappear. She panics and turns away.

"There's money buried up the deer cut," she says.

Nikki struggles to look at Billie. Her eyes are open but she can't see a thing. Now the whole world is black. She touches bone. An arm, she thinks. She tries to tunnel under it.

"Why did you keep him and not me? Why did Levi get to stay?"

Nikki's hand drops into nothing.

THEY WEAR BANDANNAS like bandits. Her and him. She is much smaller. She is five years old. They are sitting at either end of the table in the big-house kitchen and only their eyes show. On the floor in two pink piles are their insides.

Nikki jolts awake.

BILLIE MOVES HER MOUTH like she's chewing something and then she stops. Nikki glares. She throws off the chintzy comforter and sits up.

She stops in the hall and looks at a picture of Crystal hung on the wall. She's holding a baby Levi on her knee. It's one of those Walmart portraits and they're both wearing white. She looks pissed off, Nikki thinks.

The kitchen has pots and pans nailed to the wall. Even the skillet's hanging up like it never gets touched. Levi's eating dry Ramen.

"You want some noodles?" he says.

"No," Nikki says.

"Why you always carrying that bag around?"

Levi takes a bite of the squiggly block and nods at her hands. Nikki looks at the grocery bag.

"Because it's a ki of heroin."

He stares at her.

"You're holding it for your daddy?"

"No," Nikki says.

From where she stands she can see down the hallway to the bedroom. She can see across the living room to the front door. She stares at the blinds.

Before she leaves she goes in the bathroom and snags a few lollipops from the box under the sink.

"Where are you going?" Levi says.

She trudges through the yard.

COY HAWKINS is a facedown X on the bed. She thinks he is only pretending to be asleep. He would have felt her watching by now.

But when he grabs Nikki's leg she jumps.

"I'm sorry," he says.

THEY'RE WATCHING TV TOGETHER.

"What day is it?" Coy Hawkins says.

"I have no idea," Nikki says.

"Ain't school start soon?"

"School?"

Nikki looks at him.

"I ain't going back to school," she says.

"Yes, you are," Coy Hawkins says.

Nikki shakes her head.

"I got work to do."

Coy Hawkins shakes his head.

"That's over," he says.

He chins at the kitchen.

"Run get me a beer."

She stares at him in disbelief. He's covered the hole behind him. He's cut open a trash bag and taped it to the wall like she's just supposed to forget. One of his legs is hung over the side of his chair. He lifts it slightly.

"Please," he says.

She stands up from the couch and notices she is shaking.

IN THE SHED behind the big house there's a shovel.

She lugs it through the yard until the grass is waist-high. She swings it at giant weeds.

Up the deer cut, wherever there is dirt instead of rock, she slams it in. She gets down and digs with her hands. She finds earthworms and lighters and the broken-off necks of beer bottles.

At the very top of the hill all the smaller hills ripple out. They are green in the sun. They wink like they're laughing at her. She looks down at the ledge. The bloodstain's to the left. It hasn't rained once, she thinks.

There's that plywood loose on the back window of the big house. The glass is gone and she just climbs over the sill. She waits for eyes to adjust. She knows she's in the kitchen. Her kitchen from back then.

It's stripped. In the walls there are long gashes where the wiring was. Where the pipes were there are huge holes. She turns around in a circle and looks at it.

The hall creaks horribly. Her boots roll. She trips over bullet shells. The floor is covered in them. The whole place is stale with gunpowder. The stairs are gone. So is most of the second story's floor. She looks up and where her bedroom used to be there is only air.

There is nothing in here, either. Nikki puts her hands on her hips and cries for a while.

"WHERE'S THE MONEY?"

"What money?"

Coy Hawkins looks at her.

"What are you doing with that shovel?" he says.

"The money you buried up the deer cut," Nikki says.

Coy Hawkins looks confused.

"What?"

"Mama said."

"She said what?"

"She said it was supposed to be mine."

Coy Hawkins stares at her.

"And you believed her?" he says.

He lights a cigarette. He turns his head and blows his smoke to the side.

"I thought you were smarter than that."

Nikki is sweating. She's exhausted.

"There's nothing up there," he says.

She is close to his chair. She lowers her hand to the footrest and sits down.

SHE STANDS JUST INSIDE THE BEDROOM. She looks at him. He's lying on the bed. She lies down beside him. She puts her head on his chest.

He circles an arm around her, then the other one. He hugs her for a long time. She has her hand on his stomach.

She moves it to his belt. She moves it to his thigh and he tenses up. She slides it between his legs.

"Nikki," Coy Hawkins says.

He sits up.

She goes after him into the living room.

"Who are you calling?" she says.

"DSS."

"What?"

She is delirious like she has a fever. He looks at her and his whole face is winced up. He tosses his phone on the coffee table.

"There's no service," he says.

He walks into the kitchen.

FUCKING COY HAWKINS. Fuck him.

SHE WAITS FOR HIM to take a shower. He leaves his boots by his chair and his gun in one of them.

He comes out fully dressed with his hair slick at the tips. He walks by her on the couch. He goes by her again with a coffee cup. She follows him down the hall.

In the bedroom he doesn't look at her.

"What?" he says.

She shoots him in the back until the clip runs out and the gun's just clicking.

FIVE

COY HAWKINS offers his hand.

"Do you wanna dance?"

She stands from the trailer's steps. The pickup's doors are open and the stereo's blaring. She walks into the yard and he pulls her close to him. She lays her cheek on him. She can feel his breathing and his heart beating. As they sway slower and slower his beer slides from her side to his fingertips.

And then that goes away and there is nothing again, which is her favorite dream. Except it is not nothing. It is charged white space.

Nikki sits up straight on the couch. She gags and spits the lollipop out.

IT'S HOTTER THAN FORTY HELLS OUTSIDE.
Wesley's in the yard. He's with Bubba and Lee Church, who
both have shotguns. A car's growling behind them. Nikki lets
her foot off the door of the trailer.

She comes down the steps. She stops just before she gets to
them. She puts her hands on her hips and stares at him.

"Your investors?" she says.

Wesley says nothing. His mouth is slack. His forehead is
wrapped in gauze.

"Hold on," Nikki says.

She walks past them. She goes behind the big house to the
woodpile. She braces her foot against the log and pulls out the ax.

"You hear them gunshots?"

Nikki turns around. When she looks at Levi his foot skids
off the pedal.

"Yeah," she says.

She walks by them again, with the ax this time.

Inside she remembers her red eye. She finds her white sunglasses before she goes back out with the grocery bag.

She stands in front of them. She nods at Wesley's head.

"Stitches?" she says.

"What the hell happened?" he says.

"She's got blood all over her dress," Bubba says.

Nikki looks at him. She looks at all of them.

"Coy Hawkins is dead," she says.

"Holy shit," Wesley says.

"Jesus fucking Christ," Bubba says.

He lets his shotgun swing to his side.

Slowly Lee Church bends to the ground and puts his shotgun down. Nikki drops the ki at his feet.

"Let me know when y'all run out."

They just stand there while she walks back to the trailer. On the top step she sets the ax down. She looks at the door. At this moment she expected to feel something else.

She looks over her shoulder. She makes a face.

"Come on, Levi," she says.

His bike falls in the grass.

THE CARPET'S STAINED WITH BLOOD and coffee. She'll have to rip it out. But she's always hated it. Already there are flies. Nikki looks at him.

He's standing in the doorway to the bedroom. His eyes are huge. He cuts them to her. He drops the T-shirt tented over his face and nods.

"He would've ratted you out, too," Levi says.

Nikki snaps her fingers.

"Trash bag," she says.

He pulls one out of the box in his hands. He tries to give it to her but she is no longer turned to him.

"Nikki, here."

She looks at herself in the mirrored closet. She pushes the sunglasses to the top of her head. She stares at herself. She tries to be pleased by what she sees. She has to be.

"Nikki."

She steps on the body of Coy Hawkins.

"Nikki."

This is the future.

NIKKI HAWKINS raises the ax over her head.

ACKNOWLEDGMENTS

Thank you Chris Parris-Lamb, Sean McDonald, Emily Bell, Max Porter, Yuka Igarashi, my family, and, most of all, Don.

Keep in touch with
Granta Books:

Visit grantabooks.com to discover more.

GRANTA